"It's not like there's anything between us…"

With a hand on the wall above her head, Dillon leaned right down. Gloria's lids fluttered and she tilted her face up, like she wanted him to kiss her. "This sure as hell feels like something," he whispered.

"It's not," she panted back.

"Felt like more than something last night." He wanted to touch her face because there was that blush, spreading like a wildfire up from her chest into her cheeks, and he needed to know how it felt.

"It wasn't." She licked her lips in between ragged breaths.

He leaned down and for a second—maybe not even—their lips touched. Then she ducked beneath his arm and scurried to the other side of the small room.

"This will not happen again…"

Dear Reader,

I had so much fun writing *Big Sky Seduction* because it's set in one of my favorite parts of the country, Montana, where the sky is endless and the mountains stand guardian over the forests and hills. Not to mention there is something so sexy about the Montana cowboy. Dillon Cross is my ultimate hero: proud, stoic, the kind of man born of the elements, as solid as the Rocky Mountains, with spring water running through his veins. He's the kind of man who knows how to treat a woman and it doesn't hurt that he's got plenty of rope and knows how to use it. Yeehaw!

On a more personal note, the setting of this story harkens back to my youth. I grew up in a place very similar to Half Moon Creek, and our small town hosted the annual county fair and rodeo, similar to the one that takes place in the book. Would you believe that I made my rodeo debut when I was twelve? Maybe I didn't catch the greased, squealing pig as we chased it around the ring, but it was an experience I'll never forget (or repeat).

If you're from the city, like Gloria, I hope you fall in love with Half Moon Creek and its cast of quirky characters, but most of all with Dillon, because—seriously—what's not to love? (Sigh) Oh, and if you enjoy this book, watch for upcoming releases from Daire St. Denis at dairestdenis.com and like me on Facebook at facebook.com/dairestdenis.

Happy reading!

Daire St. Denis

Daire St. Denis

Big Sky Seduction

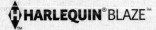

HARLEQUIN® BLAZE™

Recycling programs for this product may not exist in your area.

ISBN-13: 978-0-373-79897-1

Big Sky Seduction

Printed in U.S.A.

www.Harlequin.com

New York Times and *USA TODAY* bestselling author **Daire St. Denis** is an adventure seeker, an ancient history addict, a seasonal hermit and a wine lover. She calls the Canadian Rockies home and has the best job ever: writing smoking-hot contemporary romance where the pages are steeped in sensuality and there's always a dash of the unexpected. Find out more about Daire and subscribe to her newsletter at dairestdenis.com.

Books by Daire St. Denis

Harlequin Blaze

Sweet Seduction

_1_

OH, DEAR GOD…

Gloria's vision narrowed, like the shutter of a camera in ultra slow motion, closing in smaller and smaller. Her chest ached as if an elephant was sitting on her and a knot the size of a fist formed in her stomach.

No.

Not here.

Not now.

Carefully, she lifted the big, rough hand from her hip and rolled, or tried to, but her legs were stuck—entwined—between two large, tree-trunk-sized limbs.

"Mmm." A hand slid around her waist and snuggled her even closer to that massive chest at her back. So close, she could feel the sound of contentment rumbling against her shoulder blade, the kind of sound a big, well-fed cat of the king-of-the-jungle variety might make.

With each wriggle she made in an attempt to break free, his ridiculously powerful arms held on tighter.

"Ah, Dillon?" The words were more a gasp than a name.

"Hmm?"

She wriggled some more. No give, whatsoever. "Dillon?"

"Mmm." He nuzzled his whiskered jaw into the back of her neck, placing a sleepy kiss there. Those big, calloused hands of his roamed freely across her stomach, one up... the other down.

Gloria pushed herself away and sat up on the edge of the bed, breathing hard, as though she'd just climbed a flight of stairs, not made the simple transition from lying to sitting. Was it the dim light in the room that made her vision spotty? She rubbed her eyes.

No. It was something else.

Panting, she said, "I've got to go."

"To the loo?" He drew a line across her lower back. "Okay, darlin'. Hurry back."

Oh, God.

She stumbled—naked—to the bathroom, found the robe the hotel provided hanging on the back of the door and slipped it on. Her clutch—the one that matched the Valentine red of the bridesmaid dress that lay crumpled somewhere on the hotel room floor—sat open on the vanity counter. She checked the contents: room key, phone, lipstick and a twenty dollar bill.

Good enough. She leaned against the vanity, gulping air, willing herself under control. When she opened her eyes, her gaze landed on the cellophane-wrapped, one-size-fits-all slippers. She unwrapped them and stuck her feet inside—they were miles too big but they'd have to do. When Gloria went to stand up, her head spun and her vision closed in around her, forcing her to sit on the closed toilet seat, the bathroom suddenly a fishbowl, all watery and blurry. Closing her eyes, she focused on breathing. In through the nose, out through the mouth. In. Out. Nice and slow. Unfortunately, images from earlier in the evening decided to replay behind her closed lids to mock and taunt her.

Dillon's big, rough hands on her body. Dillon's big, talented tongue in her mouth. Dillon's big, sinfully male appendage inside of her, so…wonderful.

Wonderful? Really?

If it was so wonderful, why was she sitting here on the toilet seat on the verge of a panic attack? She hadn't had one of these suckers in years. So, why now?

It had to be the cowboy.

Gloria pressed her palms to the sides of her head to try to stop her ears from ringing.

No.

This was not going to happen.

Fumbling for her phone in her clutch, she turned it on and did her best to type a one word message—EMERGENCY!— to her best friend, Daisy. Though whether her fingers actually hit the correct letters, she couldn't tell because her phone was no more than a fuzzy shape in her hand. After a few more deep breaths, she pushed herself to her feet and careened her way to the hotel room door. She paused, listening, but all she heard was the roaring of blood between her ears.

The second she was outside in the hallway, she could breathe again, as if there was more oxygen out there. She still felt wobbly and, with a hand to the wall to keep herself steady, she lurched down the hall because it seemed that the farther away from the room she got, the clearer her vision became. Clear enough to check her phone for a reply from her best friend. Not that she really expected one.

It was Daisy's wedding night.

Shit.

She stopped in front of the elevators and pressed the button, not because she had anywhere to go, but because that was what a normal person did when standing in front

of an elevator. Except normal people didn't stand in front
of elevators naked under their hotel robe.

Good God, Glo. What were you thinking?

"I don't think I was," she whispered aloud.

The elevator dinged and the doors slid open. A bellboy was inside.

"Having a good night?" the young man asked, with a
smirk.

After a deep breath and with her head held high, Gloria entered the elevator. "Yes. Thank you." She turned to
face the front where, unfortunately, there was a mirror on
the inside of the door, forcing Gloria to face exactly the
state she was in—her makeup streaked, her pretty updo
no longer up unless sticking out in all directions was considered up.

She groaned. It was worse than she thought.

"Which floor?"

"Honeymoon suite." The words came out before she had
time to consider them. The young man pressed the button
and Gloria was subject to the longest elevator ride of her
life. She avoided his eyes by checking her phone every few
seconds, hoping for but not expecting a reply from Daisy.

How on earth had she found herself in this position?

It could have something to do with the fact that it was
Valentine's Day and her very best friend in the world just
married an amazing man and it was the nicest wedding,
ever, and while Gloria was over the moon for Daisy, she
was also a little bit…

Hmm. Jealous?

No.

Did she feel sorry for herself? Was that why she'd slept
with the cowboy?

God. That was sad.

It all started when the cowboy in question, a cousin of

the groom, got up to do his speech, but he didn't speak. Oh, no. He had a guitar stashed in the back, retrieved it and sang "Remember When" by Alan Jackson—only one of her favorite country songs of all time. She'd nearly dropped her wineglass. Instead she downed its contents followed quickly by another glass. His voice, deep and smooth, sang, *"Remember when we vowed the vows..."* It was her fantasy come to life. Except the man in her fantasy sang to her, not to the bride and groom—of all the cracked things one could imagine. Then the dance started and he asked her to dance.

She should have said no.

How was she supposed to know the man could dance?

But he could.

He led her around the dance floor, spinning her, pulling her in close, holding her tight, so sure of himself, sure of his movements, and Gloria knew, she just knew he'd be good in bed.

Stupid, stupid, stupid.

Because when he wasn't singing and he wasn't dancing, the cowboy drove her bat-shit crazy. From the moment they'd met ten months ago, when he'd purposefully done everything in his power to irk her, she didn't like him. Not one little bit. He was messy and loud and obnoxious and too sure of himself and too big and...ugh!

Every word that came out of his mouth made her want to scream. Everything he did made her want to smack him. Hard.

But, earlier tonight, while in the throes of passion, she'd let him smack *her* on the backside.

That was not Gloria. She did not do that shit.

Ever.

When the elevator finally reached the top floor of the Drake Hotel, Gloria exited with about as much dignity as a cockroach scuttling out of a room when the light came on, finding the nearest crack to crawl inside. Because of the big slippers she wore, her scuttling was more of a shuffle-slide.

"Enjoy the rest of your evening," the bellboy called.

Ignoring him, Gloria checked the screen of her phone. It was 3:17 and still no message from Daisy.

Crap.

She leaned against the wall, trying to figure out what to do. She wasn't about to interrupt her friend on her wedding night, that was for sure. But what were her options? Go back to her room? Tell the cowboy to get out?

Just like that, her vision went all spotty again and Gloria doubled over to keep from passing out. Seriously! What was it about the man that pushed her to the brink of a panic attack *just* by thinking about him? If that wasn't a sign that tonight had been a big, fucking mistake, what was?

She concentrated on her breathing again, following the advice her psychologist had given her a decade ago to keep the sense of panic at bay. But the ringing between her ears only got louder.

Wait. That wasn't between her ears, that was her phone.

"Gloria?" Daisy's voice was soft and slurred with sleep. "What's wrong? Where are you?"

"I'm standing outside your door."

"You're where?"

"Just outside."

"What are you doing there?"

"I don't know."

The phone went dead. Turning toward the wall, Gloria banged her head softly against it. This was ridiculous. Here she was standing outside her best friend's honeymoon suite, on her wedding night.

The door opened and Daisy stuck her head out. At least

her best friend looked just as disheveled as Gloria. That made her feel better. And, the fact that her friend was letting her in at all. She had to count that as a blessing.

"What happened to you?" Daisy asked, covering a yawn that looked suspiciously like a smile, as she opened the door wider.

So her best friend should be a little less amused and a little more empathetic, but whatever, she was there. Daisy closed the door, slid her arm through Gloria's and pulled her close. Gloria held on tight, appreciating the simple comfort of having a best friend when she needed one.

"How's the cowboy?"

Some best friend. "How'd you know?"

Daisy's eyes twinkled. "The way you two were dirty dancing out there tonight? Uh, yeah, doesn't take a genius."

Gloria dropped to the big white couch in the sitting area of the suite. Weird how she'd been there only twelve hours earlier, in this exact place, laughing and toasting, never imagining she'd be back. The cowboy never even entering her mind. Well, that wasn't quite true. He'd been annoying the hell out of her all day. Contradicting her, teasing her by calling her *darlin'* and *Red* and other offensive pet names. He was the kind of macho man she despised and avoided.

Until tonight.

Daisy sat next to her and Gloria realized they were dressed exactly the same, both sporting the too-big hotel robes, but Daisy's feet were bare, and her toes painted a pretty pink that matched the icing on the cupcakes that had served as Daisy's wedding cake. Focusing on Daisy's toes seemed like the only way to *not* focus on what just happened.

"Tell me…" Daisy said, patting Gloria's knee. "Is the big cowboy…*big* all over?"

"Daisy!"

This time Daisy didn't even bother covering up her laugh. "Honestly, Glo. What's the problem?"

"I did not mean to sleep with him."

"Hmm." Daisy tilted her head to one side. "Kind of looked like you did."

"I don't like him."

"You don't?"

"No. I've disliked him from the moment I met him. Remember what a jerk he was at your fund-raiser last year?"

"Of course I remember the fund-raiser. I don't remember him being a jerk. I thought he was sort of—"

"No." Gloria held up a finger to stop Daisy. "He's an ass. He may be Jamie's cousin, but he's an ass."

Daisy's brows drew together. "So, why'd you sleep with him?"

"I don't know." Gloria dropped her head to her hands. All she knew was that every time she thought of him she felt as if she was in a tiny, constricted space where there wasn't enough air and she couldn't move and she couldn't breathe and she needed to get out of there as fast as she could.

They sat there for a few minutes, Daisy rubbing slow, comforting circles on Gloria's back. "So," she said eventually. "The sex was bad, huh?"

Gloria didn't answer at first. "Well…"

Daisy's hand stopped moving. "Does that mean the sex was good?"

"No. It was not good." Gloria lifted her head to meet her friend's gaze.

Liar!

Gloria's body—the lower bits—quivered indecently at the thought of *the sex*. Dillon was certainly adept between the sheets. God, the man had owned her body yet took the time to give her pleasure, as well—more than once.

It was too much. The way he made her feel so beautiful and desirable and good. The way he'd murmured wicked things in her ear…

"Glo?"

"Hmm?"

"How come you're smiling?"

She wasn't smiling. Absolutely not.

"You're panting, too."

The bedroom door opened and Daisy's husband, Jamie, emerged, hair tousled, eyes squinty with sleep. "Wife, of less than twenty-four hours…what are you doing out here?" He rubbed his eyes. "Oh. Hi, Gloria."

Gloria covered her face and moaned. It was one thing to be mortified in front of your best friend, quite another in front of her nearly naked new husband.

"Hon," Daisy said sweetly. "Go put on some clothes."

"I am wearing clothes."

"Umm…you're wearing underwear and they really don't do a good job of covering up your husbandly junk."

Mortification did not even begin to describe Gloria's current situation. This was a mess, a royal-flipping mess, and if there was one thing she loathed above all else, it was a mess. Gloria pressed the heels of her hands into her eye sockets so hard that stars burst behind her closed lids. So much better than the alternative.

It wasn't until she heard the bedroom door close that Gloria took her hands from her face and fell back against the couch again. "I'm sorry, Daisy. I don't know what I'm doing here."

"You're obviously upset so why don't you stay. You can sleep here on the couch."

"Are you sure?"

"Of course. And if you need to borrow some clothes tomorrow morning, that's totally fine."

"I don't mean to be crashing your honeymoon."

"Oh, you're not. We've already..." Daisy wiggled her brows "...*honeymooned*. Twice."

"God."

"Plus, we're leaving for Maui tomorrow, so there'll be plenty of..." Daisy made an obscene gesture that involved hip thrusts and pounding her fist against her hand.

"Yeah, yeah. I get it. Lots of sex."

"*Lots* of sex," Daisy confirmed with the biggest grin ever.

Gloria sighed. Daisy was happy and Gloria was happy for Daisy. But she was a little bit sad for herself at the same time. Things were going to be different from now on. She was going to miss Daisy and the thought made her feel incredibly lonely.

Still not a good reason to sleep with someone, particularly one who just happened to evoke the panic attacks that you thought you'd licked a long time ago.

"Besides, you'd have done the same for me." Daisy gave her a big hug. "But, what I don't understand is, why not just go back to your room? Ask him to leave. It's your room."

Gazing directly into her best friend's eyes, she said, "Because, around that man, I don't trust myself to not make the same mistake all over again."

DILLON HADN'T SLEPT so well in a long time. Nothing like a warm feminine form to wake up to after a night of hotter-than-hell sex. He reached for the feminine form in question, with a mind to wake her up properly, a little repeat of last night's performance, but there was no one there. The bed was cold.

Huh.

He sat up, scratching an itchy spot on his jaw. Light peeked in around the drapes, revealing clothes strewn all over the floor: one sexy, black high-heeled shoe lying on the dresser, the other caught in the ice bucket. He grinned, remembering how he'd asked her to leave them on. Nothing hotter than a woman in lingerie and heels. Then he'd taken them off and chucked them over his shoulder.

Goddamn, the little redhead was a firecracker.

Now. Where was she?

Dillon pushed himself out of bed, groaning, his lower back stiffening up like it always did. Too many bulls, too many rides. He stretched side to side to work out the stiffness.

"Gloria?"

No answer.

Maybe she was in the shower.

Nice. Heat washed over him at the thought. He always loved shower sex and he was willing to bet the bossy little woman loved it, too, because—damn—she pretty much seemed to love it all.

Ambling over to the bathroom, he knocked. "Hey? You in there?" When there was no answer, he turned the knob, but there was no one there.

Huh. He scratched the same damn spot. Maybe she'd gone for breakfast. He wished she'd woken him up first. They could have ordered room service, had breakfast in bed. He would have liked to see her first thing in the morning, sex-messy, ravenous...

Hot.

He'd have liked to kiss her midbreakfast, tasting the flavor of bacon, eggs and coffee in her mouth, her skin warm as he reached beneath the covers. He'd have taken the tray away and made love to her again.

Sounded like a damn fine way to begin the day.

After pulling on his briefs and dress pants, he found his suit jacket thrown over a chair and located his phone inside. She'd given him her number, hadn't she? He scrolled. Yep. There it was, her whole name, middle name, too. He tapped a message—Where'd you go?—and barely sent it before he heard the sound of a key card sliding into the lock and the heavy hotel door opening.

With a grin, Dillon went to meet her. "Heya, darlin'. I just sent you a message." He leaned down to kiss her but Gloria turned her face to the side.

Pulling back, he took a better look at her. Her face was scrubbed of all makeup and her hair was pulled back in a simple ponytail. She was wearing some workout clothes that looked a couple of sizes too big. The result was that she looked young, fresh and innocent. Nothing wrong with that. It was the expression she was wearing that was all wrong.

Her face was pale. Her pretty lips pressed together. Her light eyes dark, as if the pupils ate up all the blue.

"I didn't think you'd still be here," she said.

"Why?"

"It's late." She looked at her phone. "Nine thirty."

"Nine thirty? Holy shit, you really tired me out." He grinned.

She frowned.

"What's up?"

"I think you should go." Her gaze was on his face but she wouldn't meet his eyes. Then her gaze traveled down, stopping at his chest before going lower. Red appeared out of nowhere, staining her neck and cheeks, making her glow as she struggled to raise her eyes. "Look, about last night. It was…"

He took a step closer and touched the red in her cheek. "Pretty frickin' amazing."

She let him touch her for a split second before stepping out of range. Shaking her head she said, "It was nothing."

"Nothing?" He dropped his hand.

"It was just sex." She bit her lip. "I probably had too much champagne."

He fell against the wall, his shoulder making a thud. Studying her close, he asked, "You telling me you regret last night?"

With narrowed eyes she said, "I'm not sure *regret* completely sums up the entirety of my remorse over last night."

Holy shit. What the hell? "So when you were crying out, coming all around me, you didn't like that?"

Her eyes were large, the same way animals looked when they were frightened and searching for an escape route. "I didn't say the sex wasn't good."

"Uh-huh?"

"I just…" Her lips parted as she breathed audibly through her mouth. "We don't like each other."

"Uh-huh?"

"At all." She waved between them. "This was just a by-product of that line between anger and passion, you know? Because you drive me crazy."

He nodded. "You did mention that once or twice. Like when I had my tongue in your pussy."

She fell against the wall, breathing hard. Kind of like last night but different. "Stop."

"What's this really about?"

She gazed up at him, pleading. "It was a mistake. Okay?" She gulped air as if it was in short supply. "So, let's just forget it happened and…" She took a long deep breath in and exhaled audibly. "Move on."

Holy hell. She was ditching him. Just like that.

"It's not like there's anything between us."

He moved away from the wall, taking a step toward her. Then another. "Really?"

"Really." The word, breathy and soft, told him otherwise, as did her wide-eyed gaze as he closed the distance between them.

With a hand on the wall above her head, he leaned right down. Her lids fluttered and she tilted her face up, as if she wanted him to kiss her. "This sure as hell feels like something," he whispered.

"It's not," she panted back.

"Felt like *more* than something last night." He wanted to touch her face because there was that blush, spreading like a wildfire up from her chest into her cheeks and he needed to know how it felt.

"It wasn't." She licked her lips in between ragged breaths.

He leaned down and for a second—maybe not even—their lips touched. Then she ducked beneath his arm and scurried to the other side of the small room. "This will not happen again."

"Why?"

"I already told you."

"None of that made sense."

She closed her eyes for a second and when she opened them, it was as though she was a different woman. Her back straightened, her eyes narrowed and pretty lips thinned. "You don't even live in Chicago. Where do you live? Wyoming?"

"Montana."

"Right." She made a hand gesture that said, *You see?* "You're what? A rancher? Farmer? What?"

"A professional bull rider."

She pointed. "Exactly!" She motioned to herself. "And I'm an interior decorator and professional stager." She forced a smile. "I bet you don't even know what that means."

"You make houses ready to sell." He said that last bit

with no inflection because the tiny woman was being con-
descending and he didn't particularly care for it.

"Okay. So you know what I do. Doesn't matter. We have
nothing in common."

He arched a single eyebrow, thinking about their amazing compatibility in the sack.

Her eyebrows drew together and a little crinkle deepened between them. "Life isn't all about sex, Dillon."

No. But good sex was a good indicator that life could
be pretty damn good with someone...

Wait a second. What was he thinking? He raked a hand
through his hair. She was doing him a favor right now.
He didn't want forever, especially not with a bossy little
fireball from Chicago. He just wanted to share some passion with someone of equal passion. After last night? He
thought he'd found it. Clearly she was looking for more.
That should be a red flag right there.

The woman bent down in front of him—a spectacular
sight—gathering up his belongings: his shoes, his shirt,
his tie, his jacket. Once she was satisfied she'd got it all,
she shoved the bundle at him. "Here."

He took the clothes. "You gonna help me dress like you
helped me take my clothes off last night?" God, he felt like
being shitty right now.

Tilting her head to the side, she said, "I'm pretty sure
you can manage."

He dropped the bundle except for his shirt. "You gonna
watch?"

"Nope." She stalked past him to the door. Before opening it, she called over her shoulder. "Be gone in five minutes. No more."

"Oh, I will be."

"Good." She stood there for a second and then called,
"Bye, Dillon."

"See ya around, Red." Dillon curled his fingers into fists at the sound of the door slamming. A part of him wanted to still be there when she got back, just to be an ass. He wanted to remind her of the fun they'd had last night, do it all over again, make her beg him to stay longer. Another part was glad she'd been so clear. He did not need to get involved with a mercurial redhead who probably didn't even think he knew what the word *mercurial* meant.

2

FAITH, GLORIA'S ASSISTANT stager and a student of Black Sect Tantric Buddhist Feng Shui—most people called it BTB, but Faith liked to say the whole damn name at least once a day—walked into the bedroom of the house they were contracted to stage, and handed her the phone. "There's a Mr. Cross on the line for you."

"Cross?" Why did that name sound familiar? She took the phone. "Hello?"

"Heya, Red. How you doing?"

Dillon Cross.

No. Just no.

She hung up and handed the phone back to her assistant.

"Who was that?"

"Some stupid cowboy from Wyoming." She pretended to go back to surveying the room when really all she could think was, why was Dillon Cross calling her? It had been *three* months. Not that she'd been keeping track, or that she'd wanted him to call. She hadn't.

At all.

The fact that he hadn't tried to get in touch with her just supported her opinion of him as a macho jerk, which was the *only* reason she'd kept track.

Faith arched a brow. "And why is a *stupid* cowboy from Wyoming calling you?"

"No reason." She made a dismissive gesture. "Now, can you help me with this bed? It needs to face the door."

But Faith was not easily distracted. Of course she wasn't. "And if it's, *no reason*, why did you just hang up on him?"

Gloria glared at Faith, the kind of expression that should tell an employee to drop a subject. But Faith was not a typical employee. "Why'd you hang up?"

"Because I didn't want to speak to him."

"Why?"

"I think I've covered that point already. He's a cowboy. From Wyoming."

"You have a very interesting aura going on right now." Faith came closer, inspecting.

The only way to distract her was to change the subject to feng shui. "It's this room. It's all wrong." Gloria indicated the cluttered placement of the furniture. "The bed's facing the wrong way, the Chi's interrupted by the big bureau. The mirror is reflecting outside. It's a disaster." She crouched down and started tugging on the bed frame. "Give me a hand. This thing is heavy."

"You slept with him."

Dammit!

She stood, wiping her palms on the front of her pants. "Maybe. So what?"

Faith tapped something into the phone, held it to her ear and then said, "Oh, hi. Sorry. We got disconnected. Was there something I can help you with?"

"Faith," Gloria whisper-yelled.

"Gloria? Sure. She's right here." Faith handed her the phone again. "Speak to him. It's the only way to clear this up." She made a fuzzy gesture at Gloria's torso. "You're all…muddy."

Rolling her eyes, Gloria took the phone but placed it next to her chest, covering the mic because Faith stood exactly where she was, waiting to listen in. She waved her off, mouthing the words, "Go away."

Saluting, Faith left and Gloria raised the phone to her ear. She took a deep breath and then huffed it out. "Dillon. What can I do for you?"

"Are you asking for real? Because the list is long." His voice was deep and suggestive. He also sounded strangely out of breath, reminding her of a very vigorous, very intimate moment she'd spent a good portion of the past three months trying to forget. So far she'd been unsuccessful.

"Why are you calling?" She bit her thumbnail, realized what she was doing and stopped.

"I'm in town, doing some business, visiting my cousins. Thought I'd give you a call. See if you wanted to get together."

"Really." She chewed the inside of her lip, realized what she was doing and stopped.

"Uh-huh. Coffee. Dinner. Or…somethin'."

"I'm not a hook-up girl, if that's what you're looking for."

"Never said you were. Just, we had some fun last time I was here," he drawled. Slow and easy. Reminding her of the movement of his tongue against her lips and in her mouth.

Mmm.

Ugh!

"Kind of hoped we could recapture it. You know?"

"No, thanks."

"Why?"

"Do you want an honest answer?"

"Yes."

"What happened between us was desperation." She gnawed her lower lip.

He chuckled. That was not the response she was going for.

"I'm not interested in whatever it is you have in mind," she hurried on.

"You don't even know what I have in mind. Aren't you curious? Even a little?"

She shut her eyes, sucking her whole top lip into her mouth while erratic visions of nakedness popped into her head.

She was *not* curious. Not one little bit. Honest she wasn't.

His voice began, soft and low, reminding her of the naughty whispers from that night. "I'm going to take your clothes off, nice and slow, kissing you as I go. Tasting every inch of you…"

No.

"Goodbye, Dillon. Don't call me again. You want a booty call, try someone else." She hung up, dropped the phone on the bed—the one that was positioned all wrong—and expelled the big breath she'd been holding.

Faith came in seconds later, obviously having overheard the entire thing. She looked Gloria up and down, shook her head and said, "You are in trouble, girl."

"No. I'm not."

Giving her another sweeping gaze, Faith's expression said different. "You want him. I can tell."

"No, I don't. Now, let's—"

"When's the last time you had sex?"

"None of your business."

"Three months ago. Daisy's wedding."

Gloria sputtered. "How'd you know?"

"Because you've been weird ever since."

Straightening herself, Gloria said, "Whatever. Now help me—"

"How about before that? Before the *stupid cowboy from Wyoming*?"

"Again, none of your business."

"Greg." Faith moved over to the bed, squatted down and began to shove, a smug expression lighting her face. "Boring, predictable, accountant Greg, right?"

"Why did I hire you, again?" Gloria tugged while Faith shoved and the heavy bed inched across the floor.

"Because I have an eye for detail." She tapped her temple. "And an amazing memory."

"Quiet and keep pushing."

"Didn't you two break up, like, a year ago? Or was it two?"

"Something like that." The bed was moving at the speed of a glacier and Gloria grunted. "How about you focus your energy on pushing instead of talking?"

Ignoring her, Faith said, "Why'd you break up again?"

"He was transferred."

"Oh, I thought it had to do with the fact he only knew one position—missionary, in the dark, no talking."

Gloria stood, giving up any pretense of moving the bed. "Look. Enough about my private life, okay? We've got work to do."

"I'll stop as soon as you tell my why you aren't accepting the *stupid cowboy*'s offer for hot sex. Because, no offense, but, you need it."

"What does that mean?" Hands on her hips, Gloria glared at her employee.

"You're wound really tight right now. A smokin' hot sex session with a cowboy sounds divine." Faith gasped and put a hand to her mouth. "I bet he has rope, too, doesn't he?" She shut her eyes and rocked back and forth, like she was imagining bondage shit behind those closed lids.

Leaning against the bed, Gloria sighed. "Enough."

"Why?"

"I lose control when I'm around him, okay? Are you satisfied now?"

Faith hugged herself. "Sounds delicious."

"No. Not delicious. The way I lose it is not a good thing." That wasn't completely true; a flash from three months ago stole her breath, in a good way. Dillon holding her legs wide while he moved inside of her... Gloria recalled feeling complete and utter abandon at that moment. However, following close on the heels of that memory was the overwhelming sensation of not being able to breathe. Of feeling constricted. Weighed down. Ears ringing, cotton balls filling her throat, heart pounding.

Panic.

It would not happen again.

DILLON JOINED HIS cousin Jamie in the locker room of the private boxing club he and his twin brother, Colin, ran. The club was frequented by Chicago's elite athletes and every time Dillon came to town he stopped in to go a round with one of his cousins. The three of them had been fistfighting for fun since they were kids, spending the summers together at his family ranch in Montana.

Funny how even as an adult, there was nothing like a good fight to take the edge off. Though that wasn't the only reason he was here. He had an appointment with Jamie who was an expert in family law.

"So," Jamie asked as he stepped out of the shower, a towel wrapped around his waist. "Gloria said no?"

"Nah. She's playing hard to get." Dillon unwrapped the tape from his hands.

"You really don't understand women, do you, Dill?"

"Are you kidding? Women are like ornery bulls and this one is doing her damnedest to make me think she wants to buck me off. But what she really wants is for me to figure out a way to ride her."

"You did not."

"Did not what?"

"Just compare Gloria to a bull."

"I like bulls."

Jamie rubbed a towel over his wet hair. "An ornery bull."

"The ornery ones are the best kind."

Laughing, Jamie said, "No wonder you can't get a date."

Dillon rolled the used tape into a ball and tossed it into the trash can across the room. "Oh, I can get a date."

"Not with Gloria. If she's decided she doesn't like you, she doesn't like you."

"Except that she does like me."

"Right."

"And she wants to see me again."

"I don't think so. Not this time." Standing in front of the mirror, Jamie sprayed some shaving cream into his palm and spread it along his jaw. "I saw her face that night. *After* the fact." He met Dillon's eyes in the reflection of the mirror. "She doesn't like you."

Dillon stripped off his shirt. "And I saw her face that night, *during* the act, and she most certainly does like me."

"Whatever you need to tell yourself to sleep at night, Dill." He made a pass with the razor, and tapped it off in the sink. "But she won't go out with you."

"You want to put your money where your mouth is?"

"What? You want to bet me that you can get a date with my wife's best friend?" Jamie laughed as he made another pass with the razor along his top lip. "I don't think so."

Dillon yanked back the curtain to the shower stall and closed it behind him. "A hundred bucks," he called as he stripped out of his shorts, turned the water on and stepped beneath the spray.

"Two hundred," Jamie called, loud enough to be heard above the sound of the shower. "That should just about cover my hourly fee."

Chuckling, Dillon used the soap in the dispenser on the wall to briskly wash off. It'd been a short bout and he and Jamie were pretty evenly matched. His jaw was still sore where Jamie'd clocked him, but he was willing to bet Jamie had some nice new bruises on his ribs. After showering, he dried off and dressed in his Wranglers and plaid shirt.

He checked out his image in the mirror, running a hand through his hair.

What was he doing here? There were plenty of good lawyers back in Montana. Of course, this was some sensitive business he had to take care of, not the kind of thing you wanted to share with just anyone, so it made sense that he'd come see his cousin, get his advice.

Then there was Red.

He'd sure as hell like to see her again. He'd planned on calling her when he first got home after the wedding, then all this shit with Kenny went down and he'd been distracted. And busy. Pretty near every waking minute had been taken up with hospital visits and looking after Kenny's ranch. It had been damn hard watching his best friend deteriorate like that. The guilt only made it worse. He hadn't had a lot of room for fun, redheaded thoughts.

But being back here in Chicago—well—his first thought upon landing was not on the will he was carrying, which it should have been, but on the redhead. Gloria-Rose Hurst. He liked the sound of her whole name.

Dressed, Dillon grabbed his jacket and the folder from

the locker and went to find his cousin who was on the phone in the little office at the back of the gym.

"The pink ones," he overheard Jamie say. "They're my favorite." Pause. "I know they don't stay on long—that's because you look even better without them but—"

Dillon cleared his throat.

"Oh. Gotta go. Love you, too."

His cousin was so *sappily married* it was hard to take. Not that Jamie didn't deserve it, Daisy was amazing, but Dillon was convinced it had to be at least partially an act. No one could be *that* in love.

"You sure you're fine to meet here, or would you rather go to my office?" Jamie asked after hanging up with his new wife.

"Here's good, if you don't mind." Dillon sat down across from his cousin and handed him a file from the folder. "This is most of it. The last will and testament of Kenny Wells."

Jamie took the folder and met his gaze. "I'm really sorry, Dill. I remember Kenny. You two knew each other forever."

"Yep." Dillon sat back in the chair, wishing he had his hat to tip forward a little. He and Kenny had been best friends, though best friends didn't do the thing that he'd done.

"What was it?"

He inhaled deeply. "Kidney cancer. Some weird strain that usually only affects men over sixty. It was aggressive."

"No kidding. Gone in a month?"

Dillon nodded. "It went undiagnosed for too long." Kenny had been complaining of back pain for over a year, but what bull rider didn't have back pain? After he finally got the diagnosis, he'd only lasted four weeks. It was as if something devoured him from the inside out. And the worst part was, that damned image of Kenny lying in the hospice bed, looking like a skeleton, was the only image he was able to conjure of his best friend after knowing him for over twenty years.

"So, you're the executor?" Jamie asked, going through the first few pages of the will.

"Yep."

He went through the rest of the document, silently flipping the pages, and as he did so a furrow formed on his brow. "Uh, Dill? You realize you're a little more than executor, don't you?"

Dillon shrugged.

"He left the ranch to you."

"Yeah."

"So, what do you need me for?"

"I don't want it."

"Why not? You weren't too keen when your parents sold your family ranch. I always thought you'd go back to ranching once you quit the circuit."

Dillon shrugged. He and Jamie were close but there were some things you didn't admit, even to those closest to you. "Nope. Too much work."

Jamie gave him a look of doubt, but it didn't matter whether Jamie believed him or not. "I need you to help me figure out how to get rid of it because I'm not keeping it."

3

ANXIETY ACCOMPANIED GLORIA on her monthly visit to her father's place. When she was still ten minutes away, the familiar symptoms reared, fire ants swarmed just beneath her skin, making her itchy and irritable. A tightness in her chest made breathing difficult and swallowing almost impossible. As she drove, she had to consciously remind herself to take slow, easy breaths so that she didn't hyperventilate.

Gloria found a spot to park two blocks from her family home in Oak Park. It had been years since she parked in front of the house; she was too embarrassed. As always, it took her a few minutes to work up the courage to get out, to overcome the urge to just drive away and never come back. She grabbed her handbag, positioned her sunglasses and hat, hoisted the bag full of frozen meals and got out of the car. She locked it and pointed herself in the direction of the house and commanded herself to walk.

Even after all these years of the house looking as it did, the sight of it still shocked her. In her mind, her family home looked as it did when her mom was still alive, back when she was thirteen. Pretty flowers in boxes and pots out front. The yard tidy, though it may have had one too many birdhouses and garden gnomes. The inside filled with treasures, her mom's collections, but always neat. Always welcoming.

She stood at the gate and stared. The shock and revulsion of the state of the yard hitting her hard—as it always did—like a sledgehammer to the gut. Bikes, old appliances, tires, toilets, garbage bags with unknown contents piled into small mountains, stacks of paint cans, lawn mowers, hundreds of broken and faded pink flamingos, wheelbarrows, thousands of broken plant pots, an ancient trampoline twisted and positioned on its side as if it had been tossed there by a tornado. In some places the trash was piled as high as the six-foot fence. In others it was only a few feet deep. There was not one blade of grass visible and the path between the gate and the front door was becoming narrower and narrower every time she visited.

Then there was the smell.

Gloria placed a hand over her mouth and nose, tears leaking from her eyes as she squeezed her way through the channel of junk to the front door. The porch, where they used to sit on hot summer days, was overrun, as well. Broken furniture, umbrellas, a shopping cart, dented trash cans.

Oh, God.

Gloria went to ring the bell, but the doorbell had been disconnected and wires hung ragged from the gaping hole. She pounded on the door.

"Dad?" *Pound, pound, pound.* "Dad, it's me. Open up. It's Gloria."

She kept her face to the door, afraid to turn around, embarrassed to be associated with whatever the hell this was. All of the overwhelming feelings of shame and humiliation from her late teens surfacing. Never wanting to be seen here. Never bringing friends home—not even

Daisy—never having a serious boyfriend for fear of what he'd think.

The fire ants migrated to her belly and chest.

Pound, pound, pound.

Her father was home. She knew he was. He'd become nocturnal, staying ensconced in his den of trash by day, only emerging at night to complete his weekly circuit of Dumpsters, searching for *perfectly good things that other people threw away.*

"Dad!" she shouted, hating that she was creating a scene.

A bolt slid, then another, then a series of chain locks unlatched and the door opened a crack. Her father's watery blue eyes stared, large behind his glasses. "Oh, Gloria-Rose. It's you. What are you doing here?"

Such a good question. Swallowing down the bile that rose in her narrowed throat, she held up the grocery bag. "Meals on Wheels," she said with a fake smile.

Her father's smile was genuine and his watery eyes teared up in delight as if she didn't do this every single month. The sight broke Gloria's heart.

"You're such a sweetheart. Come in. Come in." He opened the door wide and Gloria was greeted by a wall of stuff. Mostly newspapers, fliers and old books, piled from floor to ceiling, creating a wall of paper goods on either side. Her father lived in a massive fire trap. A coffin of stuff.

"Oh, Dad." How the hell did he live this way?

"You'll have to go in first so I can lock the door."

Gloria shook her head. She couldn't do it, the piles were claustrophobic. "Can we visit outside today, Dad? I'm not feeling so good."

He gnawed on his lip, rubbed his face and adjusted his glasses, all nervous behaviors that had worsened over the years. Before he had a chance to answer, a siren came from down the street, growing closer. Her father's already pale face went ashen. "Get inside, Glo. Now."

She shook her head and held her dad's hand, uncertain about what was going on, but having a sense that she needed to be here for this.

The cruiser stopped outside the gate followed by a city truck with a logo for Health and Public Safety on the door.

"Those bastards," her father muttered beneath his breath. "Why can't they just leave me alone?"

Two uniformed officers emerged from the cruiser. There was no mistaking the revulsion on their faces as they took in the house and yard. "Mr. Andrew Hurst?" the bigger of the two officers asked as he tried to make his way to the door, having to walk sideways in places.

"Who wants to know?"

Gloria squeezed her father's hand. Her vision going spotty as the anxiety and panic took over.

"Cook County Sheriff's Department. You're under arrest."

GLORIA SAT AT her desk, staring blankly at the computer screen. She should just go home and sleep except she couldn't, her father was there, "working," which meant he was calling lawyers and writing angry letters to the justice department about his civil rights. If he wasn't doing that he was likely yelling over the phone at some poor city clerk about the injustice he was facing.

The injustice he was facing? How about the injustice she was facing? Her whole life savings, all seventy thousand, had gone to pay his fines: five years' worth of fines for public nuisance. If he hadn't been able to pay, he would have been facing jail time.

So, bye-bye nest egg.

Yet, there was a part of her that was glad because not only had Public Health and Safety condemned the yard, they'd scheduled the house for inspection to determine whether it should be condemned, too. Which it would. The whole place was sagging.

But that meant her father would never be able to go home.

Faith came in, carrying a steaming cup of tea. She set it down beside Gloria's hand and then plopped herself into the chair on the other side of the desk. Gloria had confided some of what was going on. She'd finally had to tell someone.

"So, now what? We go over and enact a little Black Sect Tantric Buddhist Feng Shui on the place?"

There it was. Faith's daily recitation of the full, tongue twister of a name of the brand of feng shui she studied. She smiled out of habit. "I wish it were that simple."

"How bad can it be?"

"A thousand times worse than you can possibly imagine."

"I bet it's not that bad."

Gloria scrolled through the photos on her phone, found some of the best—or worst—of her dad's yard and turned the phone around so Faith could see.

"Holy shit," Faith said, her voice low with awe. She leaned across the desk and took a sip of tea from the mug she'd given Gloria. "So, what are you going to do?"

"I have no idea." She shook her head. "I love my dad. I want to help. But this is a sickness and he needs professional help. I can't pay for that sort of help and his teacher's pension sure isn't enough, either."

"Hmm." Drumming her fingers on the desk, Faith considered her. "Speaking of money, did you see the contract that came in this morning?"

"Which one?"

Coming around to Gloria's side of the desk, Faith slid the keyboard closer and tapped on the keys, opening up the office email and clicking on one that had come in early that morning. The subject line read, Montana Estate Sale, Stager Required.

Gloria read through the email from a real estate agent in a place called Half Moon Creek, Montana. A large ranch was going on the market and needed an experienced stager to prepare it for sale. The email intimated that the client was hoping to attract a certain type of buyer and had been given Gloria's name as a recommendation.

"What the hell?" Gloria asked, clicking on the attached contract.

"You know someone in Montana?" Faith asked.

"Nope."

"So where do you think they got your name?"

"I have no idea." She reread the email. "And what do you think they mean by, 'a certain type of buyer'? it sounds like code for something."

"I was just reading an article about all the celebrities who are buying up ranches in Montana."

"Like who?"

"Letterman, Dennis Quaid, Michael Keaton, Harrison Ford…"

Gloria swiveled her head toward Faith in surprise.

"What?" Faith smiled sheepishly. "So I follow celebrities? They've got nice places and people with nice places like to hire people like us." She pointed between the two of them.

"I bet it was one of the guys from the fund-raiser I threw for Daisy's bakery last year," Gloria said, still stuck on the question of who would have recommended her for a celebrity-style job in Montana.

"That could be it." Faith moved closer, reading the screen over Gloria's shoulder. "But you're not even at the best part yet. Go to the last page."

Scrolling to the final page of the contract, Gloria read through the terms of payment. "It says 2.5 percent of the sale," she murmured. "Are you kidding me? No flat rate?"

"Nope."

"Do you have any idea what ranches this size go for?"

Faith took control of the mouse and went to a file she'd been working on only fifteen minutes ago, a property comparison analysis, showing her the recent sales of ranches of comparable size and location.

"Holy crap," Gloria whispered.

"You said it." Faith's smile was wide. "And I have a feeling if we do well, get a big-time, celebrity buyer, we could get more deals like this, don't you?"

Gloria considered the situation she was in. This seemed like a godsend. But there was her father. She couldn't leave him, not alone in her place. "Maybe you should go. You've got enough experience to handle it."

Leaning over her shoulder, Faith pointed to a line in the contract. "They're asking for you, Glo. Not me. I can stay here and hold down the fort."

Leaning back in her chair, Gloria considered the possibilities. With one contract she could earn enough to float the company for six months and to give both herself and Faith a nice little bonus. If the contract led to more high-end work, they'd be set. But the thought of leaving her father alone? It didn't seem like a good idea.

With a hand on her shoulder, Faith said softly, "Your father made his mess, Glo. You've got to let him clean it up."

"I know, but…"

She squeezed her knotted shoulder muscles. "You're the child in this situation, not the parent."

Faith was right. She had to take care of herself, otherwise there was no way she could help her father. But even though that made sense logically, her heart was having a hard time with the idea.

"I'll keep an eye on your dad…and your place. I promise."

She considered the offer for a little longer, knowing she should decline it but then…what the hell? Opportunities like this only came around once in a lifetime. "I suppose it wouldn't hurt to fly out to Montana to make sure this is legit," she said finally.

"Nope. Wouldn't hurt a thing."

Gloria grinned. "Okay, then. I'll do it."

"Yeehaw!" Faith slapped her on the back. "Montana… here you come!"

DILLON AWAITED MAX Ozark's arrival. He was Half Moon's only real estate agent. He was also the mayor *and* owner of the Gold Dust Hotel, not because he was particularly ambitious but because none of his three occupations actually kept him occupied. Max had called him earlier in the day to let him know that Gloria had checked into the hotel and he'd be bringing her out to the ranch that afternoon.

Arriving early to the ranch, he saddled up one of the spirited stallions to go for a ride. Urging the horse into a trot then a canter, he rode across the expanse of grassland and up the gentle side of the bluff. It was a hot day for May and the heat led to thoughts about the fiery redhead. She'd be so out of place here where rolling hills, pastures and streams replaced high-rises. Where the Beaverhead National Forest edged the land instead of Lake Michigan. It'd be interesting to see how she handled it.

It'd be interesting to see how she handled him, too.

Would she be surprised to see him? Nah. She must have put two and two together when she read the contract. Who else did she know in Montana?

The fact she had signed so quickly and was here only a week after he'd sent it, told him one thing. For as much as Jamie claimed Gloria didn't like him, he knew differently. Not that the damn bet he'd made with his cousin mattered. Dillon had only made the bet out of habit. When they were kids, he and his cousins made bets over everything, from penny poker to who could catch a greased pig or be first to pole-vault over the creek. Chuckling, he gazed out at the Wells property, Silver Tree Ranch, it wasn't quite as big as the ranch he'd grown up on, but it sure was pretty with the hills and gullies, the forests and streams and the mountains in the distance. The Cross place, Mountain Shadow Ranch, was adjacent to Silver Tree, and Dillon and Kenny had basically become best friends because of proximity. They'd gone to school together, pulled typical teenage stunts together, started riding bulls together. That was when the rivalry started, taking the place of friendship as they vied for better times, titles and women.

Char, for example.

He and Char had dated first, then, next thing he knew, she was marrying Kenny. That had hurt more than he cared to admit and he'd still be pissed at Kenny over it if it wasn't for that thing that happened two years after they married. Then Char split, just up and left, and Dillon and Kenny reverted to being the close friends they'd started off as, never speaking of Char again.

Now Kenny was gone, and the decision about whether or not he should tell his friend about what happened was moot. It was all too late now.

When Dillon reached the old homestead, now fondly

called the Doghouse, he pulled up on the reins and turned the horse. They were standing on high ground overlooking the ranch buildings in the distance: the big log house that sat on the edge of the pond, the winding creek and forest to the west. It sure was nice. But there was no way he could keep it. He just couldn't. As long as whoever bought it kept it running like it was meant to run and made sure the hired hands who were the backbone of the place stayed on because there were fewer and fewer places for hired help to go for decent jobs these days.

With a hand to his hat, he craned his neck to check the road. Sure enough, a couple of cars were making their way along the mile-long gravel lane that led up to the ranch. If he took a shortcut across the creek, he'd make it back shortly after they arrived. With a gentle nudge with his boots and a clicking sound with his tongue, he urged the horse forward, picking a careful trail down the slope of the embankment to the creek below, making switchbacks to lessen the grade for the animal. After making it to flat ground, he followed the creek, looking for a shallow place to cross and then located a game trail through the woods that headed in the general direction of the compound.

Once the buildings were in sight, he rode directly to the barn, dismounted and led the animal inside where a ranch hand named Curtis was mucking out stalls. "Can you take care of this one for me?" Dillon asked. "Max is here."

"Sure thing." Curtis, a stoic young man of few words, looked less than thrilled at the mention of the real estate agent's name. Dillon didn't blame him.

He gave the horse a pat on its neck, passed him off to Curtis and then made his way to the end of the barn where a wash station was set up. He washed his hands and splashed cool water on his face and neck. He could almost see Gloria's look of disdain at the image he painted.

Why the hell did the little redhead's disdain amuse him so much?

Damn, he was acting like a kid about to go on a first date.

One thing was clear: he couldn't wait to see her again.

4

WITH HER PHONE in one hand and her notebook in the other, Gloria took pictures of the enormous ranch house. More like a lodge than a house, it was gorgeous. Much newer than she'd expected, too, which was a good thing because staging it alone was going to take a ton of work. She snapped another picture of the kitchen before following Max Ozark into the living room. No. Not *living room*, this was what you called a *great room*.

The vaulted ceiling was crisscrossed with wide solid beams of wood. West-facing windows lined the entire wall. She stopped to admire the view of the pond right out front with forest and mountains in the background.

"It's spectacular," she said before snapping a bunch more photos.

"It has potential," Max said, chewing on the toothpick that had been stuck in the corner of his mouth during the entire tour.

Gloria leaned against a wall, opened her notebook and added to the growing list of things that needed to be done: declutter, clear out furniture, clean windows, get new rugs, art and lighting. She made a rough diagram of the room and blocked where the new and/or repurposed furniture would go. She'd already made rough sketches of each of the eight bedrooms—yes, eight bedrooms!—plus their attached en suites. Then the enormous kitchen, the gigantic dining room, the den, the foyer, the two half baths on the main floor. Sighing, she closed the book. "What does someone need eight bedrooms for?" she muttered to herself, trying to imagine the sort of buyer they would be looking for.

"The original owner had planned to run the place as a dude ranch."

"What happened?"

"He died."

"Oh, sorry. Did you know him?"

"Yeah. He was young. Cancer." Max shook his head, sadly. "Everyone thought he was crazy for building this." He gestured toward the house at large. "Including my client. He inherited this place and probably figures it's too big to keep."

Gloria blinked and suddenly saw the place through new eyes. It was perfect for a guest ranch. "So what kind of buyer are we looking for? Someone who wants to run this as a business?"

"Either that or we find some high roller with money. Could be a celebrity type or just some bigwig corporate type who wants to pretend to be a cowboy for a few months out of the year. As long as they'd be willing to keep the place running like it is now. That's important to my client."

"What about a really big family?" Gloria turned a circle, imagining kids growing up here, adults growing old here. It seemed...idyllic.

"No one around here can afford something like this. We could throw a for-sale sign on the place and you know what would happen? Same thing that's happened to 80 percent of the places around here, one of those big corporations will buy it, leaving this brand-new house to rot, treating the land and the livestock like a factory." He shook his head. "The client doesn't want that."

"Hmm." Gloria held her pencil to her lips. "It's going to be a lot of work to attract the kind of buyer you're looking for."

"What are we talking?"

"Well…" Gloria went back to her notebook. "Everything's pretty new, but I'd like some higher-end appliances in the kitchen. Paint everything, give it a fresh look. Most of this furniture has to go and we'll need to bring in truckloads more, just to fill the place." She glanced around. "A few new light fixtures would help. Then there are all the accents, rugs, art, decorative items." She closed the book, envisioning the kinds of things she'd put in this room. "If you want a high-end buyer you need to use high-end materials. It'll be expensive and there are no guarantees."

Max nodded, walking around the room and checking it out as if trying to imagine it through the eyes of a multimillionaire. "I'll double-check with my client, but I'm sure he'll tell you to go ahead." He paused and regarded her. "The question is, are you up to tackling this sort of job?"

Excitement. That was what Gloria felt as she contemplated the challenge the ranch house presented. However, she was also a realist. "I'll be honest, Max. Back in Chicago I could do it. I've got the contacts there—contractors, furniture suppliers. Here?" She shrugged. "I don't know where to start. We're out in the middle of nowhere."

"Well, now, we may be isolated but I imagine Butte's got what you need in terms of furniture and supplies."

"What if we can't rent? Can your client afford what I'm talking about?

"We can ask."

Not for the first time, Gloria wondered who the mystery client was.

"So," Max prodded. "What do you think?"

She smiled. "I think it's an exciting proposition."

"Good, glad to hear it. You come highly recommended."

She did? She was just going to ask who'd recommended her when Max nodded toward the window. "I just saw the client ride past. Why don't we go talk over the fine points with him and then he can take you on a tour of the rest of the property."

"Sounds good."

Already Gloria's mind was spinning with ideas, a southwestern theme infused with modern touches. The log home, with its warm honey tones, would be ideal for brightly colored furniture and accents. With her head buried in her notebook, jotting down the ideas before she could forget them, she followed Max back outside to the yard.

When she glanced up, all she saw was a big man striding toward them, the sun at his back blinding her so that she couldn't make out his features.

"Hi, Gloria. Glad you came."

That voice. She recognized that voice.

Oh, no.

She shielded her eyes from the sun and his features came into focus. She pointed at him as if he was an apparition, not a flesh-and-blood man. "Dillon?"

"That's me."

"What the hell are you doing here?"

He took a couple steps closer. She stumbled back.

"What do you mean what am I doing here?"

"I mean. What. Are. *You*. Doing. Here?"

He frowned. "This ranch is mine. For now. Until you help me sell it, that is." He opened his arms wide. "Welcome."

Gloria could not believe it. She propped her fists on her hips. "You tricked me into coming here?"

"Tricked you?" Dillon tilted his head to one side, the wide brim of his cowboy hat hiding his eyes. "Is that what you think?"

"Yes, that's what I think." Gloria angled her chin up at him. Good Lord the man was big. She'd forgotten how big he was. "For what reason, I can only guess."

The real estate agent cleared his throat and Dillon turned to him. "Give us a few minutes, will you, Max?"

"Sure thing."

Dillon waited until Max was out of earshot before taking a measured step toward her. "Tell me, who did you think was behind the contract?"

Gloria bit down on the end of her pencil. "Well…"

"Who do you know who lives in Montana, besides me?"

"Oh, um…"

"Anyone?" With each step he took toward her, his voice became lower.

"I thought you lived in Wyoming," she said with a lame laugh.

"Why would you think that?"

Before answering, she took a moment to think about it. She had a vague recollection of Dillon telling her where he hailed from—twice—so why didn't she remember? She'd like to believe it was because she didn't care, but that wasn't exactly true.

God, I'm an idiot…

He frowned, as though he'd heard her unspoken words, and then he removed his hat and raked his fingers through his thick dark brown hair before positioning it back on his head.

Why did such a simple act have such a profound effect on her? Maybe it was because she was so aware of him whenever he was around—his presence, his size, seriously the man just took up too much space—it made her uneasy. So, when he spoke in that melodic, ambling drawl of his, the words just strolled right on by.

Because you're too busy checking out his package.

Oh, God! Gloria tore her gaze from the front of Dillon's well-fitting jeans. Had he caught her? It was hard to tell with the brim of his hat shading the top half of his face. She faked a scowl, hoping to cover her lapse in concentration.

"Look, Gloria. I'm selling this ranch and I need a stager. You're the only one I know."

She tilted her head back so far it felt as if her neck might snap. He was doing this on purpose, coming closer, making her feel so…small. Her instinct was to back away, but she didn't. She stood her ground. "There's this amazing thing called the *internet* and all you have to do is type the word *stager* into a search engine, and you'll get a whole list of people. It's amazing."

She may not have been able to read his eyes, but there was no mistaking the taut line of muscle along his wide jaw that told her he was clenching his teeth. Yep, he was clenching his teeth, all right, because when he spoke, it was through those closed teeth. "I may not have grown up in the big city, but that doesn't make me stupid."

"I never said—"

"No. But you implied it."

Gloria opened her mouth to refute his claim and then stopped because, while she couldn't see his eyes beneath his hat, she felt the intensity of his stare, daring her to deny the insult.

"I'm sorry."

That muscle along his jaw tightened again and Gloria found herself fighting an irrational urge to touch it, run her finger tip along it. Lightly. She clenched her hands into fists instead.

"Look, Gloria, I have no idea what I did to you to make you think I'm some asshole with an agenda. But here's the deal. I saw how efficient you were at the fund-raiser you threw for Daisy. According to Jamie, you pulled that event off in less than a month. You're organized, professional and experienced. You can get the job done and that's what I need."

The last bit was said so low, the words threatened to sift through her hair before floating by on the wind. Gloria wasn't even sure she heard him right, all she knew was that the sound of the letters strung together evoked a tingling sensation at the base of her spine.

Dillon's gaze slid from her to take in the surrounding landscape. "And, I want this place sold as soon as possible."

Gloria got in her car, started up and drove away. God, what was wrong with her? Why was she acting like such a jerk?

Dillon. That's what was wrong with her. There was something about that man that drove her insane, something about him that got under her skin and made her completely crazy. She took a deep breath and blew it out very slowly.

Well, at the very least, this time he didn't bring on a panic attack. That was a good sign. Why she'd had one the last time, she still didn't understand because there'd been no reason for it that made any sense. It had been years—four at least—since her last one. What had that one been about?

Oh, yeah.

She'd gotten trapped in an attic when moving furniture up there for one of her jobs. The small constricted space, full to the rafters with junk, one second she was fine, the next she was on all fours, barely able to breathe. Thank God Faith had been there.

While this one hadn't been a full-blown attack, Gloria knew how these things worked: the *fear* of an attack would linger at the back of her mind, festering, reminding her that she was powerless and she'd be living with low-grade fear that an attack could come on at any time, any place, undermining her tenuous sense of security.

Making her feel weak.

Out of control.

It was the worst feeling in the world.

She glanced up into the rearview mirror, watching the buildings of the ranch grow smaller in the dust from the gravel road and she increased the pressure on the gas pedal.

So the contract hadn't worked out. At least it gave her some time away from Chicago to gather her thoughts. With this contract off the table, what she needed to do was put her head down and get to work. But she couldn't go home. Her dad was there, and while she loved him fiercely, his manic energy would not be conducive to her well-being. It never had been.

Maybe she should see if she could stay with Daisy for a while. No. Daisy was still a newlywed, she didn't need to be crashing that party, as if crashing their wedding night wasn't bad enough. Sighing, Gloria racked her brain, going through her list of friends, ticking off who she could possibly stay with. But there was always something: new baby, marriage trouble, new job, no room…

She'd ask Faith, except living together and working together was never a good idea.

What she needed was a holiday.

She couldn't afford a holiday.

Unless she stayed in Montana…which wasn't exactly a holiday.

Gloria's foot weighed heavily on the accelerator and the rental car flew across a single lane bridge over a meandering creek and then back to the road. Fields, pastures, hills and sky painted watercolor portraits in her peripheral vision.

For a fleeting second, Gloria felt wild and free.

Until she hit a patch of gravel and the car started to slide, almost as if it was winter and she was driving on ice.

"Shit!"

Gloria tugged the wheel and the back end fishtailed as she overcorrected one way and then the next. Time slowed and things became clear: the sound of spraying gravel, the thudding of her pulse through her body, the impossibly blue sky and stark peaks flashing past the window.

Was this the moment of clarity that came before death?

If so, there was a peacefulness to it that seemed out of sync with the utter chaos of what was happening around her.

5

"I CAN LIST it as is," Max Ozark said, already snapping shots of the yard and barn with his camera phone.

Dillon barely heard him. He was eyeing the progress of the line of dust traveling away from the ranch.

"Dillon?"

"Huh?" He turned his attention back to the real estate agent.

"Do you want me to list it?"

Rubbing his jaw, Dillon surveyed the property. "Yeah, I guess I do."

"I can take a bunch more outdoor pictures while I'm here."

"Sounds good." Dillon pointed to the place where he'd ridden earlier in the day. "You can get a nice panoramic shot up on the bluff over there. Take one of the quads or a horse if you like."

"I'll take a quad. You know me—I like my animals four-wheeled."

"City slicker."

Max laughed. "Speaking of, what'd you do to piss off the redhead?"

"No idea."

"Women."

Max was speaking from experience. Father of five girls, three of whom were married with kids. All girls. Dillon had gone to school with the eldest of them.

"Look, you finish up here." Dillon handed Max the extra key he'd had cut. "I'm heading back to town. Got some things to take care of."

"You're not staying out here till it sells?"

"Nah."

Focusing on the image on his phone screen, Max said, "Thought you might—you were always staying on when Kenny needed help."

"Yeah, well." Dillon adjusted his hat so it sat more firmly on his head. "I helped when I was around. Kenny didn't have much in the way of family."

Max looked as if he wanted to say more, but kept his mouth closed, for once. He was a good guy, but loved his gossip, and the fact that Kenny Wells had left the ranch to Dillon was fodder for a town that was always looking for something new to talk about.

He climbed into his F-350 4x4, supposing the latest speculation was that he and Kenny were gay. He chuckled and rubbed his chin at the utter ridiculousness of that thought. Not that he cared what other people did or who they loved—live and let live, and all that shit—but the thought of him and Kenny?

He quickly replaced the thought with one of Gloria. He could still see her as clear as anything, the way she looked lying underneath him: her fiery hair spread out all over the pillow, her pretty lips parted, her eyes closed as flashes of pleasure radiated across her face. Now, that was a fine image to have emblazoned in one's memory. There were others, too. Gloria's face turned up to him, smiling wide, throwing her head back and laughing as he led her across the dance floor. That image might be even clearer because that was the moment when he'd decided he needed to take her to bed. A woman who had the ability to let go, to dance with such abandon and laugh with such freedom was a woman he wanted to make love to.

The thing he couldn't quite figure was what happened to that woman. Where did she go? It was as if he made her up because the woman he woke up to—scratch that, she'd left before he'd woken up—was different. She was cold. Distant. Bossy.

She was…

"Shit!"

Dillon geared down and pulled over because the woman in question was in the ditch standing beside her car, looking a fright and holding her cell phone up as though she was hoping to get hit by a bolt of lightning. He pulled the truck over to the side of the road, parked it and got out. "You okay?"

Without answering his direct question, she said, "I can't get a signal out here at all."

He indicated the miles and miles of grazing country. "There aren't many towers around here."

She swore beneath her breath and Dillon covered up his smile by kicking the front tire that was bent at an awkward angle and ducking down to check underneath the front end. He stood, dusted his hands on his jeans and said, "Your front axle's bent. You need a tow."

Her hands were on her hips and she was staring at him, her lips pressed together, as if it was his fault. Or maybe not, because that was when he noticed how pale her face was and the remnants of fear lingering in her clear blue eyes. Moving slowly, the way he approached a newborn colt, he said, "I'll give you a lift to town. Walt's got a truck at the service station. He can tow it back."

Her lips moved as though she was going to say something and then stopped. She nibbled on her bottom lip. "You sure? I don't want you to go out of your way."

"Darlin,' it's either that or you walk back." He moved to the driver side. "I'm going to town anyway. Hop in."

As if she had a choice—which she did not—Gloria looked around for other options.

Dammit, the woman was starting to make him mad.

"If you're so dead set against riding with me, you can wait for Max. He should be along in an hour or two. Or, you could go back to the ranch and grab a horse. Ride back to town." He didn't even bother keeping his skeptical smile in check, the image of Gloria…bumping along on an old nag, well that was good for a laugh. But when she still didn't get in the truck, he climbed in, started it up and rolled down the passenger side window. Leaning over he said, "Get in, Gloria. I don't bite."

She grabbed her things and got in. Staring straight ahead, she said, "Thanks."

"My pleasure."

Sneaking a glance at him while he pulled away, she added, "That's a lie, you know. I remember quite clearly. You do bite."

Dillon's low chuckle vibrated around in the cab of the truck as they sped down the bumpy gravel road. What had possessed her to say that? She'd vowed she wouldn't bring up their night together and at the first opportunity, she reminded him—and herself—of what happened. Not that she needed reminding. What she needed was to forget.

"I wasn't the only biter that night."

She laughed. Then stopped herself. It wasn't funny.

But when the truck's back end fishtailed along a particularly "gravelly bit" of road and Gloria pressed her foot against the imaginary brake pedal on the passenger side while her knuckles turned white on the armrests, she suddenly forgot everything but the road ahead. "Can you slow down a bit?"

He glanced over at her. "Not used to gravel, huh?"

"I never would have guessed it'd be so slippery."

"Yep. Can be tricky if you're not used to it."

"So, um…can you please slow down?"

"I've driven on these roads all my life. I know them like—"

"Please."

Instead of finishing what he was going to say, he slowed down.

"Thank you."

"No problem."

Gloria stared out the passenger window, trying to think of something to say to fill the awkward silence. Her brain played over all kinds of possibilities except none of them were appropriate: *Do you have a girlfriend? Do you still think about me? Why didn't you call?* She finally settled on the first appropriate thing that popped into her head. "So why are you selling your ranch?"

Without taking his eyes off the road, he said. "It's not mine."

Had she misheard before? "I thought you said it was yours."

"It was my friend's. When he passed, he left it to me."

"Your friend left you his ranch?" Gloria turned in her seat. "Wow. You must have been very good friends."

"Since we were kids," he said without emotion.

The bright sun came out from behind a cloud, shining in and lighting Dillon in a way she'd never seen him before. She studied his features—at least those she could see—square jaw covered in short whiskers just around his mouth and down to his chin. Full lower lip. His nose was nice, with a slight bump on the bridge. Dark hair peeked out, curling up beneath his cowboy hat.

What color were his eyes? Brown? She couldn't remember.

"You done?"

"Excuse me?"

Never taking his eyes off the road ahead, he said, "You done staring?"

Shit. Gloria covered up her faux pas by asking another question. "Why don't you want it?" Did that sound suggestive? She hurried on to say, "The ranch, I mean."

The same muscle that had twitched earlier along his jaw tightened right back up again. "Ranches are a lot of work. This one still has a hundred and fifty head of cattle, about a dozen horses. That's a lot of care and maintenance. I'm on the road pretty much year-round—rodeo circuit and all."

"Oh."

"Plus, taxes and the upkeep on a place that size are astronomical."

"I bet."

"Cattle prices are always fluctuating. It's hard to make a go of it."

"Gotcha." But Gloria didn't quite get it because it sounded as if Dillon was trying to convince someone other than her of the reasons why he didn't want to keep the ranch. And seeing as there were only two of them in the truck…

Plus, that muscle along his jaw was all tense again. Then again, the guy's friend had died. She couldn't forget that.

She cleared her throat and said softly, "I'm really sorry about your friend."

He nodded.

"What was his name?"

"Kenny."

She chewed on the corner of her mouth. "What happened? If you don't mind me asking."

In a detached voice, Dillon proceeded to explain how his friend had been diagnosed with a rare form of kidney cancer that took him fast. "Came home from the wedding and found out. He only told me because he needed help with the ranch while he was going through treatments." Dillon shook his head. "Treatment never helped. Made him weak. It was probably too late anyway." His nostrils flared as he took a slow deep breath. "He passed a month ago," Dillon finished.

That's why he didn't call after the wedding...

"I'm so sorry."

Gloria realized she was staring at Dillon's profile again, at the firm set of his jaw, the granite stoicism of his cheeks. He didn't look sad, he looked...mad? Pissed off, maybe? Why would he be mad? Was he still upset with her?

Though she hated to admit it, she had been a bitch, treating him in a way he totally did not deserve.

"Um, Dillon?"

"Yeah?"

"I need to apologize."

"What for?"

"My behavior. Back at the ranch..." She drew a deep breath and blew it out. "After the wedding."

For the first time since they'd gotten into the truck, he turned his head and eyed her from beneath his hat. "Okay."

Somehow, Gloria's thumbnail found its way between her teeth. She removed it and sat on her hand. "I kind of..."

When she didn't continue, he asked, "Kind of what?"

"Freaked."

He frowned. "Why?"

"I don't know."

"And by 'freaked' you mean…?" His words trailed off as he waited for her to explain herself.

"I used to get these…episodes."

"Like a seizure?"

"Not really. But…" She shrugged. "They come on suddenly and I have no control over them." She hazarded a smile in an attempt to downplay the traumatic effect the attacks had on her.

"And being with me brought one on?"

She caught her lower lip between her teeth. "Yep."

He really wasn't watching the road now. "Damn, Red. Why didn't you say something?"

She laughed and then caught herself. A panic attack wasn't a laughing matter so why the hell was she laughing? "I was embarrassed," she explained. "Plus, I never thought I'd see you again. I didn't think it'd matter."

His lips turned down at the corners. "So you thought it was okay to treat me like an asshole?"

Her automatic response was to deny it. But he was right. He was the first man to really light her on fire and she'd been downright rude to him. "I guess I just wanted to make sure it wasn't going to happen again." She twisted her hands around one another. "I don't want it to ever happen again. The episodes," she clarified. "So, I need to be clear that *this*—" she motioned between them "—isn't going to happen again."

He nodded once. "Who the hell says I want it to happen again?"

Wow. It was exactly what she wanted to hear, exactly how she hoped this conversation would go, and yet the words stung.

"Good," she said. Not meaning it, not even a little.

"Glad we cleared that up."

CONVERSATION CEASED AFTER they'd established how things stood between them. Was he playing games with the city girl? Maybe. But Dillon needed her and if she thought all he wanted was to get her back into bed, then she'd be hopping on the next plane back to Chicago and he didn't want her going back to Chicago.

Plus, seeing her in shock by the side of the road, well there was just something about that damsel-in-distress thing that pulled at his sense of obligation. Not that Gloria-Rose—why did he always think of her in those terms—was a damsel in distress. Quite the opposite. In fact, he'd practically had to pick her up, throw her over his shoulder and carry her off for her to get in the vehicle with him.

An image of doing that very thing waltzed through his mind, spinning and turning, taking him back to the wedding.

Well, one thing was certain, he wasn't going to pressure her. That didn't mean he wasn't going to do his best to seduce her. That'd be fun. The thought of tempting her and getting her to be the one to decide when they'd fall back in bed together sounded like a fine idea. Hell, the best idea he'd had in a long time.

Schooling his thoughts, he navigated the familiar road back to town and drove straight over to Walt's Full Service where Walt was out in the yard, playing fetch with his dog. They explained the situation and Walt promised he'd tow it first thing.

"How long will it take to fix?" Gloria asked.

"A couple days at least, depends if I can fix the axle or need to order one."

Next stop was the Gold Dust Hotel, one of Half Moon's original buildings, harkening back to the gold and silver rush days. It still had the best food and saloon around, which wasn't saying all that much.

"Thanks," Gloria said, hand on the door handle, ready to leave.

"So," Dillon said, before she could open the door. "You still interested in the job?"

Their gazes met and the shock of her clear blue eyes, made brighter by the sun slanting in through the window, resulted in a tightening in his gut and lower parts. Why did the woman have such a visceral effect on him? He hadn't felt this way about a woman since... Char.

"I need to think about it."

"What do you need to think about?" Dillon dug his hands into the wheel of the truck to keep from reaching for a strand of flaming hair that fluttered around her head in the breeze of the open window. Silk. He remembered the texture—couldn't forget, in fact—it was like fine silk.

She gnawed on the corner of her lower lip. "Nothing." Her mouth smiled but her eyes didn't. "My car's going to be here for a few days at least. I'm not going anywhere soon anyway." She forced a bigger smile, this time showing some teeth. "We've worked things out...between us, right?"

Dillon suppressed the grin that wanted to break free. "This is a business relationship. Nothing more."

"Good." She rubbed her palms against the front of her dress pants. "Now that we've got that sorted, there's no reason why I shouldn't stay."

"No reason," Dillon added.

"Okay. Then, I'll see you later." She stepped down from the truck. "Oh, and Dillon?" She leaned in through the open window. "I guess I'll need a ride out to the ranch tomorrow."

"Sure thing, Red."

Her eyes flashed, as he knew they would, but she didn't say anything about his pet name for her. Dillon drove off, giving in to the grin that split his chops.

6

GLORIA WANDERED DOWN the main street of Half Moon Creek looking over her shoulder for cameras and staged gunfights. The place was like a Western movie set. Seriously. It couldn't be more Old West if it tried. Was it a mistake to take the contract? Maybe. Maybe not. It didn't really matter now. She was here, she was stuck and she needed the money. End of story. This thing between her and Dillon? It was manageable. She'd gotten Dillon's word that nothing would happen between them and she could control herself around the man. Hell, she'd even managed to control herself when he'd called her Red.

As she walked, she passed a café, the Bank of Missoula and, across the street, a town hall and square. After walking past a Laundromat and a hardware store, Gloria stopped. She gazed in through the window of a shop called Mesa Verde Furniture, Decor and More. As she entered, a little bell jangled. Standing in the doorway, Gloria gazed around in awe. Here in the middle of nowhere was a beautiful store filled to overflowing with southwestern decor: furniture, rugs, lamps, throws, candles, wall hangings and everything a decorator could want. She wandered toward the back where there were knickknacks. So many things, perfect for furnishing the house.

"Excuse me?" Gloria called as she approached the woman behind the counter who was organizing crystals on a shelf behind her. She wore a full, multicolored broom-stick skirt and loose cotton blouse and had gray hair plaited in a braid down her back.

"Oh!" The woman finally turned around, a wide bright smile lighting her weathered face. "I didn't hear you come in." She had the most interesting eyes, so light they were probably gray but almost appeared white.

"No problem." Gloria smiled in reply to the woman's warm expression.

"What can I do for you?"

Gloria leaned forward and described what she wanted—to be able to rent furniture from the shop in order to stage the ranch house. "If a place is staged well, with the right furnishings, the buyer often asks for furnishings included. So you'd get the rental as well as the sale price. What do you think?"

The woman drummed her fingers on the countertop, but then her face split into a grin. She stuck her hand out. "I think we have a deal, Gloria."

Shaking her soft hand, Gloria asked, "How did you know my name?"

"Oh, honey, you're not in Chicago anymore."

DILLON MADE HIS way up to the bar. "Hey, Beth," he said to the woman behind the counter, who was an old school-mate and happened to be the eldest of Max Ozark's girls. "Bud, please." He pointed to his favorite draft pull. As Beth poured, he asked, "Did Lacy lose her tooth yet?"

"Last night." Beth smiled. "But the little rascal was

determined to stay awake for the tooth fairy. So the poor fairy didn't get a lot of sleep."

He grinned. "Being a fairy is hard work."

"You said it." She slid the cold glass across the bar to him, leaving a wet streak in its wake. "You know what the word is around town these days, don't you?" She leaned her elbows on the bar, her eye alight with mischief. "Talk is, Char ran off because there was something going on between you and Kenny the whole time." She covered her mouth to suppress her laughter.

"I was wondering if that was the rumor."

She shook her head. "Not that anyone cares."

"Right."

"Only Reverend Harness."

"Uh-huh."

"You could have done worse than Kenny. He was a good guy."

Dillon picked up the pint. "To Kenny." He drank deeply.

"To Kenny," Beth repeated before wiping the moisture off the countertop. "Of course, then there's Chicago over there." Using her chin, Beth pointed to a table in the corner where Gloria was sitting, eating what appeared to be a salad and drinking a glass of white wine.

"You have wine?"

"I'm as surprised as you."

He grinned. The sight was just so…wrong for Prospectors Saloon. Dillon turned back around and rubbed his jaw to keep from laughing.

With her elbows on the bar top, Beth said, "People are wondering about your relationship with her, too. It makes for some interesting speculation."

"Good Lord." Dillon tilted his hat back. "People need to get a life around here."

"Aw, c'mon, Dilly Bar. You know how it is. We need to

be entertained. You're it at the moment. By the time the county fair comes around I'm sure there'll be something else to talk about. Mickey Donaldson will get drunk and light a fire. Eric and Addie will break up but get back together before it's all said and done. You know how it goes."

"Uh-huh."

"You hungry?"

"Already ate."

"Singing tonight?"

"Thought I might."

Beth looked at her watch. "We'll get started in half an hour. That work?"

He nodded. Picking up his beer, he said, "Guess I'll go feed the rumor mill." He ambled across the wide-slat, wooden floor to where Gloria was seated. "Heya."

"Hi."

Was it his imagination or was there a pretty pink stain creeping up Red's chest, continuing up her neck to her cheeks? Damn, he never thought blushing was sexy before.

"May I join you?"

"Sure." She indicated the empty seat with her salad fork and moved a notebook out of the way so he could set his beer down.

"How's the salad?"

Crinkling her nose, she said, "A little wilted, to be honest."

Dillon laughed. "Well, it's not really the Prospectors' signature dish."

"No? What is?"

"You're in cattle country, darlin'. What do you think?"

Shrugging, she sipped her wine and crinkled her nose after that, too.

"Steak and beer, babe."

"Of course." Setting the glass down firmly, Gloria said, "Please don't call me 'babe.'" She paused. "Or 'darling.'"

Lifting his hat off his head, he ran a hand through his hair before replacing it. "Won't happen again, Red." He pressed his lips together, waiting for her to say something about *Red*. She didn't, though the comment deepened the color in her cheeks.

She straightened her shoulders. "What are you doing here, Dillon?"

"You might have noticed this is one of the few places in town to eat."

She pointed at his beer. "You're not eating."

He lifted his pint to her. "Very astute." Using his raised glass to point, he indicated the six-foot-by-six-foot raised stage in the opposite corner. "Open mic tonight."

"You're singing?"

"Thought I would."

She blinked rapidly, lifted her wineglass and polished off what was probably a skunky wine, based on the expression she made. "That's nice."

Huh. Something had gotten Red riled. What was it?

"So." She kept her eyes downcast as she moved salad around her plate. "I spoke to Walt. He says he's got to order parts. Could take a few days."

Dillon nodded. "That's what I figured." He nudged the notebook. "What's this?"

"My plan of attack."

"And what might that be?"

"First step is declutter. And with a place the size of that ranch, that's going to take a lot of work. Part of that is eliminating at least half of the furniture. You'll have to decide what you want to keep and what you want to get rid of or sell."

"I'll probably give away most of it. There's a Quonset where we can store stuff until I figure that out."

Gloria watched him closely before turning her attention back to the list in her notebook. "After we've cleared the space, we'll want to paint and fix anything that needs fixing. We also need to refinish the floors and maybe update the kitchen appliances, that kind of stuff."

Dillon nodded in acceptance while his brain was shouting, *Holy shit!* That was a ton of work, way more than he'd bargained for. There went his idea of just sticking a for-sale sign up on a fence post and being done with it.

"I did some market comparisons and there seem to be a number of ranches available in this area. If you want to sell, you have to set yourself apart. Attract the right kind of buyer. Max was telling me that you're interested in the celebrity type."

"I don't really care as long as whoever buys it actually runs the place. Max is the one jostling for a celebrity." Dillon didn't feel like explaining he wanted something different for Kenny's ranch than what had happened to his family's place.

"I'm going to need boxes to pack things. Usually I bring in a Dumpster for all the throwaway. A place like this could use two or three." She paused to take a long drink of water.

"The dump is twenty miles away—we've got trucks to haul stuff. I can get the boys to help."

"Okay." Gloria used the menu on the table to fan herself.

"What's wrong, Red? You hot?" Even though he hadn't intended for his comment to be sexual, it came out sounding that way and he wasn't the only one who realized it. Gloria's already rosy cheeks heated up a notch and Dillon had to squelch the urge to lean over and press a kiss there, tasting her heated skin.

Gloria cleared her throat and said, "I…ah…stopped into a store down the way. Mesa Verde?"

Without skipping a beat, she was all business again. "Oh, yeah?"

"I spoke to the owner."

"Sage?"

"Yes."

"What did you talk to her about?" Sage Morningsong was a Half Moon fixture, her great-grandmother heralded from the Crow Nation, her great-grandfather, Charlie Spencer, was one of the founders of Half Moon, though Sage adopted her ancestors' maternal last name. She and his mother had been close, and to this day, Sage invited him for supper at least once a week. She was an interesting woman with all kinds of weird and wacky stories, and Dillon enjoyed her company. It didn't hurt that she was a great cook. But, she also had this way about her that made him uneasy, like she knew things she had no business knowing. Not that Sage was a gossip—it was more like she *saw* more. *Sensed* more. Knew exactly what was what. What he'd done. Who he was. What he was thinking.

He realized Gloria was still talking, explaining how she wanted to rent furniture to stage the house. It sounded fine by him. He liked the idea of keeping business local and the stuff in Sage's shop was nice. It'd look good in the house.

"I already picked out a few items. A couple of sofas, some chairs. Some art."

Tipping his hat at her, he said, "You move fast."

"If I'm here to do a job, I'm going to do it."

"Good, and I'll pick up what I can and take it out tomorrow."

Gloria folded the paper napkin—as if it was some kind of fancy cloth thing—and stood up. "Guess I'll head up, then."

"You're not going to hang around?"

She sucked a corner of her lip into her mouth. Damn. It was adorable and hot as hell, reminding him of the greedy way she sucked on his lips back in that hotel room in Chicago.

"I'm tired."

"Right."

"It's ten o'clock back home. Time difference."

"Uh-huh."

"Okay, then."

He stood because that was what you did when a woman was leaving the table, but the gesture seemed to surprise her and she took a step toward him, tilting her head to gaze up into his face. Sweet mercy, the urge to reach for her, to draw her into his arms, was overpowering.

"See you tomorrow," she whispered.

"Uh-huh." He removed his hat. "Sleep well, Red."

GLORIA DID NOT sleep well. The walls of the old hotel were paper-thin and Dillon's voice floated up through the night air as if he stood right outside her window serenading her. She could even itemize every song he sang.

"The Thunder Rolls," by Garth Brooks. "Then," by Brad Paisley. "Through the Years"… Kenny Rogers.

Only some of her favorite songs by some of her favorite country artists, except sung in Dillon's deep, rich voice. Her imagination went wild, picturing him propped right beside her in bed, shirtless, muscles rippling as he hugged the guitar, playing it as though it were a woman he was making love to. Yep. Sleep was not in the cards when her mind was so intent on playing out dirty, sexy fantasies featuring Dillon Cross.

She didn't even have to make shit up. All she had to do was *remember* because the memories were closer to the surface than she'd like to admit. The taste of Dillon's mouth, warm and wet. The feel of his short beard against her cheek, against her thighs. His talented hands, sometimes gentle, sometimes rough. Who knew calluses could be the source of such immense pleasure?

She shivered.

"What the hell am I going to do?" she whispered to herself.

Do him, was the answer.

Gloria scooched down beneath the thin sheet. The air in the hotel room was warm—she should probably turn on the air conditioner, except the hum might drown out the sound of Dillon's voice. She reached a hand beneath the band of her panties and slipped a finger inside.

Wet. Just thinking about him had her drenched.

Oh, this was bad.

Finally, Dillon handed the microphone to someone else, it was a female. Who? The pretty bartender that had made him laugh?

She flipped over in bed. It was eleven o'clock her time but it didn't matter. Tired as she was, sleep was a long way off. So, she got up, opened her laptop and created a new file using her 3D interior design software. Work was the only thing that was going to take her mind off Dillon.

7

THE NEXT MORNING Gloria was roused by a ringing telephone beside the bed. It took her a few moments to orientate herself and to figure out where she was.

"Hello?" she said, her voice thick from disuse.

"Heya, Red."

"Dillon?"

"Yep. You up?"

"Where are you?"

"Downstairs. You ready to go?"

Shit! What time was it? The clock on the bedside table read eight o'clock. That couldn't be right. "Give me ten minutes."

"I'll give you twenty."

Gloria had the fastest shower of her life and then went through her suitcase to find something suitable. Today was going to be a physical day, moving furniture, cleaning—she needed to wear comfortable clothes. Plus, according to her weather app, it was going to be warm. Yoga pants and a T-shirt would have to do. She pulled her hair back into a ponytail and applied her makeup.

She was downstairs with five minutes to spare. That gave her time to grab a coffee and muffin from the restaurant. When she went back out to the lobby, Dillon was there, leaning against the front desk, talking and laughing with the woman who worked there. She looked a lot like the bartender from last night, maybe a few years younger. Pretty in a wholesome girl-next-door sort of way.

When Dillon saw her, he straightened up to his full, ridiculous height and a low, steady throb pounded through her.

"Morning, Red."

"Dillon." She nodded at the girl behind the counter who was pretending to be busy with the computer but Gloria had already seen she was playing solitaire.

Dillon held the door for her as they went outside. The back of his truck was piled with furniture, covered in tarps and secured with rope. "Wow. You don't mess around."

He opened the truck door for her. God, when was the last time a guy had done that?

"There's a time to get busy and there's a time to mess around. Critical thing is to figure out when to do what."

She didn't know how to respond to that so when he put his hand out to her to help her up into the truck, Gloria took it. Not because she needed the help—good Lord it was a step up and she was wearing yoga attire—it was simply an automatic response.

There was no denying the response she had to touching his hand again. The calluses brought back every dirty image she'd fantasized about the night before. Her nipples tightened as if he'd rubbed the callous pad of his thumb against them. Her thighs twitched with the phantom memory of his calluses brushing sensitive skin in that general region, as well.

"You okay?" Dillon asked. "You sound like you're out of breath."

"I'm fine." She turned toward the passenger window,

lest Dillon be able to read her thoughts as well as hear her increased breath. "Thanks for picking up the furniture."

"No problem."

They rode in silence the rest of the thirty miles to the ranch. After she got her wandering, dirty thoughts under control, Gloria gazed out the windows and noticed the landscape. It really was beautiful country around here. Wild. Untamed. She could almost imagine what it must have been like for the first explorers to have discovered it, and she was willing to bet it really hadn't changed much since Lewis and Clark's time.

"You grew up in a beautiful part of the country," she said, just as they turned onto the lane that would lead them to the ranch.

"I think so. But then, I'm biased." Dillon backed the truck up to the porch that surrounded the log house and parked. They climbed out and went around back to the tailgate, which he lowered. "Let me see if Curtis and Thad are around to help unload."

"I know I'm not much to look at, but I am pretty used to carrying furniture," Gloria said, hands on hips.

Dillon took in her body with his gaze. Down, up, down—pause—up. "Not much to look at? Red, have you looked in the mirror lately?"

Gloria couldn't remember ever being made to blush so easily and it, more than his comment, made her mad. "I can carry furniture."

He ignored her because he was whistling to get the attention of the ranch hand who was walking toward the barn at that very moment. "Curtis, over here."

To Gloria, he said, "Maybe when you don't have help, it makes sense. But you've got help, so use it. You're the expert. We're the grunts. You tell us where to put the stuff and that's what we'll do."

It made sense, yet for some reason, the fact that he was right made her even madder. Or…something. It wasn't as if she was *mad*, she was—too busy to figure out what she was because the two men weren't only strong, they were efficient. Much more efficient than she and Faith would have been…damn them.

They moved in a couch, a love seat and a chair and left them covered in a corner of the room. Then Gloria pointed out the furniture that needed to be removed, which was most of it.

Hands on his lower back, Dillon nodded, though there was no mistaking the look of pain that flashed across his face.

"I'll get Thad to help," Curtis offered. "You two move it out, we'll carry it to the Quonset."

THIS WAS THE last of the furniture for today. Dillon rose slowly, his back hollering at him. After the beating his spine had taken over the last decade of bull riding, all this bending and lifting was killing him. The doc had told him to do yoga to help strengthen and stretch the muscles around the damaged vertebrae. Any more riding and he'd be looking at surgery.

There was no way in hell Dillon would be caught dead doing yoga.

Though, if it meant he got to hang around with a woman like Gloria, wearing that tight yoga outfit, where every dip and curve was in plain view for his eyes to explore and feast upon, well, hell, maybe it wasn't such a bad idea, though he preferred the kind of yoga a man did without clothes.

"Storm's going to hit any minute," Curtis said just as a gust of wind nearly stole his hat, whipping one way and then another, the air dropping ten degrees in a matter of minutes.

Dillon grabbed for his hat, holding it in place when a streak of lightning split the sky followed by an almost immediate ground-rattling roll of thunder. Within two more steps, big fat drops of cold rain kicked up little divots of dust in front of their feet.

"It's here already," Thad said, stating the obvious.

"You going to hit the road or wait it out?" Curtis asked.

"I'll see what the boss says."

Curtis swept his long hair out of his eyes only to have it blown back again. "I like her."

"Me, too."

By the time they got back to the house, they found Gloria had set out a meal for them in the dining room: cold cuts, pickles, biscuits, cheese. Beer. Considering no one had lived at the house for months, it didn't surprise Dillon that she'd been able to make a meal out of what was in the larder. Most folks in these parts stocked their pantries for the apocalypse, even Kenny, apparently.

"You guys have been working hard all day, you need to keep up your strength," Gloria said. "I know it's not much but I hope it'll do."

Dillon was so touched by the effort he moved up close and leaned down to whisper, "Any reason I need to keep my strength up?" For not the first time today, he caught the scent of fresh laundry on her. It had to be his favorite perfume.

She turned and he'd swear there was playfulness in her gaze. It quickly hardened, but there was no doubt about it, Red was a day and maybe a beer and a half away from bantering right back...or more.

"Because if memory serves—" he dropped his voice even lower "—you require a good deal of stamina."

There it was—the sweetest sight. A delicate pink hue appeared between the straps of her top, climbing her neck as if it was the face of a mountain, inch by inch.

A millisecond later a bolt of lightning lit up the room followed quickly by a resounding crack and the lights went off. It wasn't late enough for it to be dark out, but the low clouds made it feel later than it was and the house darker than it should have been. Luckily, there were some candles on the sideboard in the dining room and Thaddeus pulled out his lighter and lit them.

Was it wrong of Dillon to wish the two other men away so he could sit there and share a romantic meal with Gloria? Curtis seemed to get the hint, quietly mentioning to Thad to head on back to the bunkhouse. But the weather had put Thad in a storytelling mood and somehow the fire got lit in the great room and the four of them ended up sitting around on what was left of the furniture, shooting the shit while Mother Nature put on a light show to rival the Fourth of July.

"You ever seen a mountain lion, Miss Gloria?"

"No." Gloria's eyes were wide as she listened to another of Thaddeus's stories.

"City folk think bears are the ones to fear out here in the hills. Nope. Bears are more like us than we think, most of 'em just wanna be left alone to dig grubs, fish, find berries, that sort of thing. More people are killed by cows every year than bears." Thad scrubbed a hand down his face. "The big cats on the other hand? They're predators through and through. Stalking. Watching. If they attack, they attack for a reason. Purposeful. Why last spring, there was a big ol' cat that decided it wanted Sue."

"Who's Sue?" Gloria asked, leaning forward.

"The resident mutt that follows Thad everywhere," Dillon supplied. He could see Gloria's mind working as she frowned, wondering what happened because she hadn't seen the dog around.

"Did the lion get her?"

"Well now, let me tell you what happened…"

Dillon sat back and crossed his ankles, getting comfortable. Originally from Louisiana, Thad had the storytelling gene and could make a trip to the hardware store into an epic tale on par with Homer's *Odyssey*, rife with trials, tribulations, sirens and adventure.

"Now this cat had its eye on Sue. A sly thing, more cunning than any that had come around these parts before. Patient, too. Watching from afar, like it was taking note of her daily habits, storing all that information in its predator's brain. But more than that, too. Like it was personal.

"To watch Sue, a guy'd a thought she had no idea she was being stalked. But I knew. Didn't I say as much to you?" Thad pointed at Curtis who nodded reluctantly. "She a clever one, our Sue, and she wasn't about to be outsmarted by some other critter that was skulking around her territory. You know what she did?"

"No?" Gloria said, obviously engaged in the story.

"She pretended she was hurt, limping like she'd torn her paw, making the cat believe she was an easy target. When the cat pounced, it was too late. Sue had lured it right into a big ol' cat trap I'd set up. *Snap.*" Thad clapped his hands for emphasis, making Gloria jump. "And that was the end of that cat."

"Is that true?"

"Darn tootin'. I've got a cougar skin rug at the foot of my bed to prove it. Sue sleeps on it most nights."

"Where is Sue now?" Gloria asked.

"Coyotes probably got her." Curtis's lips twitched.

"Naw, she's out on a walkabout at the moment. She'll be back, mark my words." Thad rubbed his hands together.

"Now, there's got to be a guitar around here somewhere. Curt?"

Curtis got up and found the instrument leaning against the same wall as the fireplace and held it out to Thad who shook his head and pointed at Dillon. Dillon gave it a strum and began tuning it when Gloria stood.

"It's getting late. We've got a long drive back to town and this storm doesn't seem to want to let up."

Setting the guitar down, Dillon pushed himself to his feet, keeping his groan inside. "I've got to get the generator started before we leave."

"Curt'll take care of it," Thad said. "You two better head out before it gets too dark."

GLORIA RACED THROUGH the torrential downpour for the truck, using her notebook over her head as an umbrella. She would have rather stayed in the house, listening to Thad tell tall tales in his thick Southern accent, sitting beside Dillon, sneaking peeks at him while he sat there. God, she longed to hear him sing again.

But that was not what she needed.

What she needed was to do the job and go home. The fact that Dillon was so helpful today moving furniture around, despite the obvious pain in his back, not putting up a fight when she had him declutter most of the main floor, made her fondness grow. She'd been expecting him to pull something like he did at the fund-raiser last year where he seemed to want to undo everything she'd done. He hadn't.

"Spring storms can be nasty," he said, as he started the truck up and got the windshield wipers going. "With snow still in the mountains, water levels can rise quick."

Gloria didn't trust herself to speak because she had too many warm thoughts toward him right now. When she didn't comment, he leaned in and turned on the radio, fishing for a station that wasn't all crackle and settling on a local talk-radio station.

Within seconds, an alert sounded and an automated voice came over the radio: "A severe weather warning continues for all of southwestern Montana, including Beaverhead, Deer Lodge, Granite, Madison, Jefferson, Ravalli, Gallatin and Silver Bow Counties. Power outages, hail and flash flooding have been reported in Beaverhead, Deer Lodge, Silver Bow…"

The weather alert continued and Gloria glanced at Dillon, whose face was almost invisible, lit only by the console lights in the truck. Inky blackness surrounded them and the headlights only cast light so far. It was as if the road only existed a few yards in front of them and at any moment they'd be driving off the edge of the world into nothingness.

Suddenly, a large, dark shape appeared by the side of the road. Then another and another.

"Shit!"

Dillon's sudden expletive, combined with him slamming on the brakes kick-started Gloria's pulse.

"What is it?"

"Bridge is out." He pointed ahead where the small one-lane bridge had been. In its place was a torrent of water. "A fence must be down, too, because the cattle are out roaming." He put the truck in Reverse but the tires just spun. "Dammit." He popped the truck into four-wheel drive and backed up slowly before managing to find a spot wide enough to turn around.

Suddenly the already scary storm took on a whole new level of darkness as Dillon sped back to the ranch, the windshield wipers moving at a harried pace across the windscreen, not doing a bit of good.

"What are you going to do?"

"We need to get the cattle to higher ground. With them all down in that low spot, they're in danger of getting caught in the flood, particularly with all the new calves." He cursed beneath his breath. "The thing about a herd is they like to play follow the leader, even if the leader decides to go and get its dumb self drowned."

The two hands must have seen the headlights of the truck coming back because they came running across the yard and met Gloria and Dillon under the overhang on the porch. Dillon gave them the lowdown on the cattle.

"Is the road passable?" Thad asked.

"Nope. Nearly got my 4x4 stuck."

"Best take horses." Thad kicked the ground as though he was mad at it. "Dammit, we need a few more hands to wrangle that herd. They're probably split on both sides of the creek."

"It's more like a river than a creek now."

"I'll go get the horses saddled," Curtis said.

"Make it four," Gloria shouted to be heard above the pounding rain.

Dillon frowned at her. "I appreciate the offer, Gloria, but this isn't the time for a horseback lesson."

"I'm a good rider. Let me help."

"That's not a good idea."

"Why?"

"This is unfamiliar territory. You'll be riding an unfamiliar horse. I don't need to worry about you *and* the cattle."

She knew what he was thinking, that she'd sat on a horse a couple of times on holiday and now thought she knew how to ride—which was not the case at all. There was no time to argue and only one way to get him on her side. She had to show him.

Stepping right up to him, she said, "You don't need to

worry about me. Saddle one up and I'll show you. If you still don't think I can ride after we hit the edge of the yard, I'll come back."

Gloria could see all three men weighing the need for a fourth over having some city girl from Chicago being a liability when things were already dire.

Dillon rubbed the whiskers on his jaw. "Okay. I'll let you show me if you can ride. But you've got to promise to come back if I say so. No argument."

"I promise."

8

As much as Dillon liked Red, now was not the time for this shit. In fact, by the way the other two were grumbling and Thad was cracking his knuckles, they thought it was nuts, too. He just hoped she'd be quick about it and abide by the promise she'd made, coming back to the house after she found she couldn't keep up.

Though the woman did seem to know how to work the straps on the stirrups, shortening the length to fit her. That was an unexpected development. And she sure as hell looked cute with that big oilskin jacket swallowing her as she sat astride, but there was no mistaking the expression of unease as she settled into the saddle.

When her gaze met his—which was no doubt skeptical—she squinted and said, "I'm used to an English saddle, but I'm sure I'll get used to this." She patted the saddle horn. "It's a lot bigger, that's for sure."

Of course. City woman would ride English. She made a soft clicking sound and maneuvered the horse in a circle toward the door. Okay, so the woman managed to direct the gelding out of the stable, that didn't mean she'd have the first clue how to ride in a storm with a bunch of scared cattle doing whatever the hell they wanted while floodwaters threatened to sweep them all away.

"Where'd you learn to ride?" Dillon asked as he caught up with her.

"I spent every summer at horse camp after my mom died. My dad…" She pulled the collar of the jacket closer. "Well, I loved it. It was the best part of my year." She smiled and the next thing Dillon knew, Gloria took off, riding circles around him, spitting up mud as the circles narrowed in closer and closer, showing off just how much control she had of the horse, moving with the animal as if it was an extension of her body.

Damn.

Then, for all that was holy, the woman turned the horse and headed full tilt for a low fence.

Dillon envisioned the horse putting on the brakes and her going headfirst over the horse and fence, landing hard on the other side and breaking her neck. He kicked his horse into a run, his heart in his throat as she picked up speed the closer she got to the fence. Then, all be damned, woman and horse flew right over the fence, and the two of them landed soft and easy, as though they'd been jumping together for years. She circled once more before riding right up to the three of them—three stunned men—probably all carbon copies of one another: eyes wide, mouths open.

"Damn, girl." Thad rubbed his cheek. "That was something else."

"That was more than horse camp," Dillon said.

She shrugged. "I used to compete. It's been a while but," she said, pausing, "the second I saw this horse, I could tell he was raring to go. He's got lots of energy, like he hasn't been ridden in a while." She patted the animal's neck. "We're going to get along just fine."

CONSIDERING HOW WARM it had been earlier in the day, Gloria was now chilled to the bone. It must have been almost midnight by the time they managed to get most of the cattle to high ground. The four of them had split up, Thaddeus and Curtis working with the half on the east side of the ranch, where the ground was low and more treacherous. She and Dillon had come around the west, forging higher ground and corralling the herd on the other side of what had been a creek—something she could have jumped across on the back of the gelding—and now was a raging river of mud and debris.

Considering the treacherous conditions created by the storm, they'd only lost one cow. It had been caught in the mud and Dillon had done his best to rope it and get it out, but the rope kept slipping and the mud sucked the animal down while water rushed right up and over it. She'd heard cows low before but this poor thing had made a sound like she'd never heard from a cow. A scream that sounded almost human.

When Dillon's horse stopped, she was so lost in her thoughts she almost rode right on by.

"Gloria, hold up."

She stopped her horse. Dillon was sweeping the beam of his flashlight over the inky black landscape ahead. "Is something wrong?" she asked.

"See that?" He moved the beam up the slope and down. In the darkness it looked like tar, black and slick. "Mud slide. Might be unstable. Definitely not good footing."

"What do we do?"

He stood in his saddle and shone the beam up and behind them. "Well, there's always the Doghouse."

Gloria was game for many things, but there was no way in hell she was sleeping in some doghouse.

"Follow me. Move slow. Who knows how stable this section of ground is."

Moving her horse right up behind Dillon's, Gloria barely had to control it. The animal that had been so full of energy earlier in the evening was tired and willingly followed in the footsteps of the stallion Dillon rode. They carefully picked their way up the slick slope, until they came to a small plateau. Dillon shone the flashlight ahead and it lit on a dark, rectangular shape.

"This is it."

The Doghouse looked like a building out of one of those Old West towns: squared logs with white chinking, the wood worn and gray, and a small porch. Dillon rode around back where there was an open-ended outbuilding—a shedlike structure—that sheltered firewood and was large enough for a couple of animals. After dismounting, Dillon turned to help Gloria, but she'd already kicked her leg over and was stepping down, groaning because her muscles cried out from the cold and from sitting astride a horse for hours.

She was going to be sore tomorrow, no doubt about it.

They unsaddled the horses and removed the bridles of the tired animals, stacking the saddles and saddle blankets on some logs to air out. Without any grooming implements, they couldn't do more than pat the animals down. Dillon spoke softly to both horses, as if thanking them, and after a final pat, he gestured with his head for her to follow him. She kept her eyes down, hoping he wouldn't notice the sudden moisture pooling there.

It must have been the exhaustion.

The steps leading up to the house were sturdier than they looked and once inside, Dillon used his flashlight to locate some dry matches to light the gas lanterns: one on the table in the center of the room, the other on the mantel above the fireplace. With the lanterns lit, Gloria could see the place and it was tidier than she'd expected. Obviously it had been in use more recently than the outside facade suggested.

"What is this place?"

"The original homestead."

"It's in good shape."

"Yep. Been used by all the Wells men ever since Kenny's great-grandfather first settled in this area."

Throwing her head back, Gloria laughed, more a product of exhaustion than of humor. "The Doghouse. I get it."

"Also doubles as the local gambling hall. When there were a lot of hands working this ranch and the next one over, the men would all meet up here once a month to play poker." Dillon bent down—slowly—in front of the fire. Opening a wooden box that contained kindling, he arranged the material in the hearth before lighting a fire.

"Huh." Gloria said, taking in the place: the wide, wooden slat floor, a rock fireplace charred black by smoke on one wall, and an old-style wood-burning cookstove took up another wall. A ladder led up to a loft, where she imagined there was a small sleeping area.

With a large metal bucket in his hand, Dillon said, "There should be plenty of water in the rain barrel. I'm going to water the horses, then I'll heat some up so we can wash."

"Sounds good." Warm water was exactly what she needed, she was soaked through. Gloria shrugged out of the too-big oilskin jacket and hung it up on a peg by the door. She moved closer to the fire, which was already crackling in the hearth, and held her cold hands up to the warmth. Dillon was back seconds later and he, too, removed his big jacket and hat and hung them up by the door. Then he came toward her, bucket in hand, eyes reflecting the jumping flames.

"Have I told you how much I appreciate your help tonight?"

"Not yet."

He smiled but didn't actually say thanks. Instead of joining her by the fire, he went to a shelf, found an old sooty kettle, opened the lid, blew into it as if blowing out dust, and then poured rainwater inside. There was a hook embedded in the stone of the fireplace and he hung the kettle there before finally turning to her. His lazy gaze swept down her body and back up, making her shiver even though the fire was throwing off plenty of heat.

"Nice bra."

"Huh?"

"Darlin', that wet T-shirt of yours leaves *nothing* to the imagination."

Glancing down at herself in horror, she realized her white tank top was completely wet and completely seethrough, making her baby-blue bra *completely* visible.

"May as well take it off to dry." He took one more step toward her and leaned down. A drop of water fell from his hair onto her cheek. "No need to be shy. It's nothing I haven't already seen."

A shiver snaked down from where the water droplet trickled as if it was liquid fire, warming her cheeks and neck as if she was sunburned.

"Need help?" Dillon asked as he started to unbutton his own shirt.

"No." Gloria shook her head, droplets flying from her wet hair.

With a chuckle, Dillon shrugged out of his damp shirt and hung it on the back of a chair, leaving him wearing a white cotton undershirt.

From an old trunk that sat beside a rocking chair, Dillon removed a wool blanket and brought it over to her.

"Here." He handed her the folded blanket.

"Thanks," Gloria mumbled. She turned her back and tugged the shirt up and over her head before wrapping the blanket around her shoulders. The fabric was a little scratchy and smelled of wood smoke.

"Don't think I'm trying to get you naked, but…"

She glanced over her shoulder and his slow grin contradicted his words.

"You might think about taking off those pants, too. They must be soaked."

Turning away again, she bent low, keeping the blanket around her shoulders, draping herself so that she could remove her yoga pants. Even though the oilskin was long, it hadn't kept the rain off her legs and the stretchy material was sopping wet. When she turned around, Dillon was bending over himself, kicking off his boots and pushing his jeans down his thick, muscular legs.

She gasped and then covered her mouth. If he'd heard her, he didn't let on.

Once straightened, he hung his jeans over another chair and held out his hand for her wet garments.

"Your undershirt's not wet?"

"Now who's trying to get who naked?"

Her abdomen fluttered with unexpected tugs of memories and desire. She knew what was under that T-shirt. Solid, freakin' muscle. A couple of scars. Two or three tattoos, a few that were peeking out from his short sleeves right now. She swallowed hard because her mouth was watering so much.

"Now that you mention it, my shirt is wet." Crossing his arms in front of himself, he gripped the edge of the T-shirt and brought it up and over his head. The simple movement was the sexiest thing Gloria had ever seen; rippling ab muscles greeted her first, followed by well-defined pecs with curls of dark hair in between. Then there were the man's shoulders: wide and powerful, so, so masculine. Holy hell. It would have taken something on the level of a natural disaster—of the flash flood variety—to get her to rip her gaze away.

Dillon, on the other hand, seemed to find her fascination with his body amusing because he smiled in that slow, easy way of his and then turned around, presenting his firm backside outlined through the thin material of his boxer shorts as he rooted through a cupboard.

God, she wanted him.

There were no two ways about it, she wanted to remember what it was like to be with Dillon Cross. Seeing him in his underwear, practically naked? Well, she was on the verge of running over there, warming her cold hands on what she was sure was smokin' hot skin, throwing off her blanket and tackling him.

When Dillon turned, he had a bottle of whiskey and two glasses in his hands. But he stopped and met her gaze. "What are you thinking about, Red?"

Gloria swallowed and tugged the blanket tighter around her shoulders. Not trusting her voice, she did a combo head shake and shrug, to say, *Nothing.*

"Okay." He held the bottle up for her to see. "You like whiskey?"

"I don't know. I don't really drink it."

"Well, I'd offer you some other beverage but that's all we've got. Oh, and a tin of tea that's been there since 1905."

"Whiskey it is, then."

Dillon blew into the glasses, same as he'd done with the kettle, before filling them. "Here," he said, holding out the glass. "This'll warm you up from the inside."

"Thanks," Gloria said, reaching for the glass with both hands. The second her fingers touched his, she took in a sharp breath and her blanket fell from her shoulders.

Standing still, as if cut out of stone, nostrils flared as if he was taking in her scent, Dillon said, "Red, you are hard on a man's self-control."

Setting the glass down on the big table, Gloria stooped to retrieve her blanket. She secured it around herself, picked up the whiskey and took a gulp. The liquid singed the back of her throat and left a trail of liquid fire down her esophagus and into her stomach. "Holy shit. That is strong," she sputtered before taking another drink.

He watched her for a second and she realized how nice it was to see his features so clearly without the shade of his hat, particularly in the flickering firelight. She loved the way shadows leaped across his gorgeous chest as it rose and fell, and how the fire made his eyes dance. The air was thick between them. Smoky maybe? Or something else.

Definitely something else.

Slowly, without breaking eye contact, Dillon lifted the glass to his lips and drank all of its contents. Then, just as slowly, he set the glass down and took a step toward her. Followed by another. And another until he stood directly in front of her. With him standing so close, she could smell his skin, the rain, the remnants of aftershave mixed with the salty scent of man. Gloria had to tilt her head way back to look up at him, and her gaze traveled from the hollow of his throat, up the tendons of his neck to his jaw and finally his eyes.

There was sin in those eyes. Deliciously playful. Contagiously wicked.

It made breathing difficult, thinking impossible. When not given direction from her brain, parts of her body started acting out: her hands reaching for the bare skin of his abdomen, her tongue running the length of her lower lip, her nipples tightening against the damp satin of her bra, her thighs clenching to keep the throbbing sensation under control.

"Gloria." He said her name so low it was almost inaudible.

"Yes?" She became fascinated with how her hands appeared against his skin, marveling at the fact that she was really touching him after secretly imagining it for months.

Based on the substantial bulge, barely hidden behind the cotton of his shorts, he was enjoying her touch. Except he took her hands away and squeezed before setting them aside.

The unexpectedness of his actions punted her out of her fantasy. "Sorry," she said. "I don't know what came over me."

"Don't apologize." He moved to the fireplace and, using an old rag to protect his hand, removed the kettle from where it hung and carried it over to a shelf where there was a wash basin and poured the steaming contents inside. "Have a bit of a wash, you're covered in mud."

"Oh."

"And when you're done, we'll pick up where we left off."

9

Was it wrong to watch Gloria wash and find it incredibly sexy? The way she bent over the basin, her pale skin like fine china, the curve of her bare calves and ass, the way her bra barely seemed to hold her breasts?

No. It was right.

Being here with her, seeing her so comfortable in a way he'd never for the life of him expected? Dammit, nothing had ever felt so right.

"Your turn."

She wrapped herself back up into the blanket and went to sit by the fire. Dillon took the basin that was now murky with dirt and tossed it out the open door before refilling it again and going through his own washing up procedure. She was watching, too.

That made it even more right.

So what the hell was making him hesitate?

I freaked. I have these episodes. It can't happen again.

All valid reasons for him to keep his distance except that in this cabin, distance was pretty much impossible. After washing, he retrieved another old blanket from the chest, gave it a sniff—passable—and then pulled up a chair next to Gloria. "You comfortable?"

"Mmm-hmm." She glanced at him, smiled shyly and then turned her gaze to the flames in the hearth.

"Gloria?"

"Yes?" Eagerness. That was what he identified in her voice and it gave him hope. "I can't tell you how much I appreciate your help tonight."

"Thanks for letting me help."

"You're a fine rider."

By the way she lit up, it was as if he'd given her the best compliment in the world. She sucked on her lower lip—heaven help him—and said, "I want to thank you, too. You were a big help to me today."

"Well, I have a vested interest."

"Of course. You want the place to sell."

He didn't nod or acknowledge her statement, instead he pulled her chair close—so close their knees were touching—leaned forward, slipped a hand behind her head and kissed her.

She fell into him, thank God, her hands going to his shoulders gripping. Lord, her lips were soft. So nice and soft and her mouth tasted of whiskey. She groaned and tilted her head, which he took as an invitation to kiss her more deeply.

So he did. Tangling his tongue with hers, sucking that suckable lip of hers into his mouth, greeting her inquisitive tongue by sucking on it, too.

Heaven. That was what she was. A little slice of heaven after a hellish night.

"Dillon?"

He stroked the hair at her temples, loving the texture of it. "Yeah, baby?"

"I want you."

With a groan he set his forehead against hers. "You sure?"

"Yes."

Standing, he pushed his chair out of the way, threw the blanket on the floor in front of the fire and then loosened her blanket from around her shoulders, baring her top half. The cabin had warmed up but, by the goose bumps on her forearms, she was still cold. Well, he knew exactly how to warm her up.

Moving around behind her, he swept her damp hair out of the way, placing a kiss on the back of her neck, tasting her skin, softly first, running his lips along the cords made taut by the tilt of her head, licking her, sucking her. When her head relaxed against his arm, he gripped her shoulder harder, biting, gentle at first, harder when she started to moan.

When he began to suck in earnest, she cried out, falling back against the chair. With his hand in her hair, he moved her head to the other side, giving the newly exposed part of her equal attention, sucking on the tendons that stretched before him, licking the hollows created, up to the base of her jaw, breathing heavily in her ear before tasting that small shell as he sucked her lobe into his mouth.

"Dillon…"

She tried to turn toward him, but he didn't let her. He kept his fingers threaded securely in her tangled hair, holding it off her neck so he could kiss the back, brushing first with his thumbs and then tasting, scraping with his teeth, rubbing his whiskered jaw against her skin. She had the most beautiful long neck, delicate and yet strong, too. He couldn't get enough. Tugging on her hair, he pulled her head back, exposing the front so that he could lean right down over her and suck on the most tender part of her throat beneath her chin.

"Oh." Her voice was soft and breathy as she reached around behind for him. "I've never…no one's ever…"

"Shh." He ran the pad of his thumb over her lips to silence her because the minute she asked him to do more, he would be too weak to stop the flood of desire he felt for her. He knew from experience that, while Gloria might say she wanted him, he did not want a repeat of Chicago, where she gave him the cold shoulder the next day. So this time, he was going to make damn sure she knew what she was doing.

SHE COULDN'T BREATHE. Not because of a panic attack but because Gloria had never been more turned on. She'd thought that thing that happened between her and Dillon in Chicago was an anomaly, the product of too much wine and wedding emotions. It had been the kind of sex she'd always dreamed of having but never thought was real. Sex like that was something that was created for movies and books. *Real* people didn't *really* feel that way.

Dillon had just proved that assumption wrong for the second time.

Leaning her head against him once she finally caught her breath, she whispered, "Wow. That was…" Gloria was going to say "amazing" but *amazing* didn't quite describe how his lips and tongue and teeth had made her feel. Phenomenal? Out of control? While he held her head tenderly against his abdomen, stroking her hair back, she tilted her head up and back. "What do you call that?"

"Necking."

"My God," she whispered. "I like your version of necking."

"I'm glad because you have the most beautiful neck."

She rose in front of him, her blanket left behind on the chair. She had tunnel vision but it wasn't panic cutting off her peripheral vision, it was desire that had her focus on one part of Dillon at a time. His narrow waist where his boxers rode low, for example. Touching him there, she watched her fingers caress his skin as if they belonged to someone else, moving back and forth along the waist-band. He had the nicest abs, so hard, his skin so soft. And the line of hair that separated left from right was so deliciously masculine. She drew her finger up and down, up and down, fascinated by the way his muscles constricted on each ragged inhalation.

With the backs of her knuckles, she skimmed up the muscles of his stomach to his chest, turning her palms flat against him and leaning in to press a kiss right between his well-defined pecs. She rubbed her cheek there, needing to touch him with all her parts, needing to feel as if she wasn't removed from this, wasn't just watching, but was fully taking part. With the side of her face pressed against him, she inhaled deeply, breathing in his still-damp skin as she plastered herself up against him. Skin to skin somehow wasn't close enough. She wanted more. Needed more.

"Your bra's wet."

"We should take it off, then." She reached around behind her and undid the clasp.

Dillon kissed the straps off her shoulders, moving lower as the bra slipped, revealing her nipples before tumbling to the floor.

"You are so beautiful," he spoke from the deepest part of his chest, a rumbling erotic sound that was as good as a caress.

When he bent to take a nipple in his mouth, Gloria let her head fall back, arching in encouragement. There was something so freeing about giving herself to this man, finally doing what she wanted, being the person she wanted to be.

Uninhibited.

Sensual.

Alive.

The suction increased and residual embers from the whiskey reignited flames in her belly, spreading up into her chest and down through to her toes, causing her knees to weaken, forcing her to dig her fingertips into Dillon's gloriously broad shoulders in order to keep herself upright.

"Do you have a condom?" she asked, her practical side surfacing.

"In my wallet. In my jeans."

"Get it."

As much as she didn't want Dillon to move out of her embrace, she knew what she wanted and she didn't want to have to stop later in order to make it happen. She'd never been so bold with a man, asking for what she wanted, telling him to go get a condom.

Just do me.

Who was she?

Gloria never had trouble telling people what she wanted in business and in life in general. But in the bedroom? She'd always been reserved, fearful of showing too much. Afraid of asking for what she wanted. What she needed.

"Come here, you." After finding what he needed in his wallet, Dillon took the blanket from the chair and spread it on the floor on top of the other one. When she was close enough, he held her hand and pulled her down to her knees. Caressing the side of her face he said, "You sure about this?"

"Dillon. You've already asked me."

His expression became serious. "I know but…"

Oh, God. He was afraid she was going to freak out again. That was why he was being so careful. That was why he kept stopping just when he got her going. She squeezed his hands. "I want to make love to you, okay?"

He gazed deeply into her eyes, as if he needed confirmation from more than just her brain and voice but from her soul. A deep-seated shiver ran from the base of her spine up to the top of her head, not a chill, but a pleasant, liberating sensation.

"Please."

That one word was like the chink in his dam of self-control. His heavy lids fluttered closed and he groaned as he yanked her flush against him so that he might close his mouth over hers. The passion and attention he'd paid to her throat was now focused on her lips, the inside of her mouth, her tongue, sucking, nipping, biting. It was the kind of kiss Gloria had always hoped for. Better even than last time.

She wrapped her arms around his neck and pulled him down on top of her. She wanted to feel his weight on her because his size made her feel so small and feminine. She needed to feel him skin to skin, needed to be as close to him as physically possible. The desire to be as close as two individuals could be was all consuming; a need almost as dire as breathing.

She must have Dillon inside her, penetrating her, just like his tongue was doing right now, pushing past her swollen lips. She wrapped her legs around his waist, positioning his erection in order to tell him what she wanted. When he went to roll to the side, she held on with a ferocity she didn't know she possessed.

"I must be crushing you," he whispered hoarsely.

"No. You feel good."

"Mmm, darlin'. You feel incredible."

"Take off my panties."

Hoisting himself to his knees, he slipped his fingers beneath the band of her panties and she lifted her hips to help. Once they were off, she wantonly let her legs fall open.

He sat back on his heels, taking in her exposed flesh. "Beautiful."

And that was how he made her feel. Beautiful.

"Take off your shorts."

He tilted his head to one side. "Darlin'…"

"Please."

Apparently *please* really was a magic word, one Dillon was unable to say no to. With a groan, he rose to his feet and pushed the band of his shorts down his hips and over his massive thighs.

"Don't move," she said, rising up in front of him.

"Damn, you're bossy," he replied with a wicked grin. Not to mention a splendid erection. The man was incredible. While she'd been naked with him before, it had been dark in the hotel room and she hadn't had a chance to really look. Standing there in front of her? Dillon Cross was…beautiful.

"You had your fill yet?"

"Come here."

His eyes lit with a wonderful combo of amusement and desire as he took a step forward.

"Give me the condom."

He handed her the plastic square. "Damn, woman, I like you bossy."

"Mmm. Glad to hear it," she said, ripping the plastic and removing the slick disk from inside. Kneeling before him—God, he was so big and beautiful—she took a hold of his shaft and slowly rolled the condom over him.

Dillon made a sound that was half hiss, half growl and he dropped to his knees, pushed her onto her back and spread her legs in order to fit himself between them. Carefully, he eased his weight on top of her as he took her hands, threaded his fingers through hers and raised them above her head.

"You drive me crazy," he whispered, rubbing his jaw

against her cheek as his hips made slow circles between her thighs.

Lovely, wonderful friction.

But Gloria needed more than friction, so much more. She turned her face and lifted her chin, positioning her mouth flush against his. With a groan, he seared her lips and simultaneously ground his erection against her mound.

"Please, Dillon," she whispered into his open mouth.

He slid his hand down the length of her arm, down her side to her hip before fitting his hand between them. "I need to touch you first."

"No."

"Yes."

His fingers found the top of her, prying her open. He slid one, and then two fingers, inside.

Gloria's body reacted with the joy of penetration, going rigid as if electrocuted with a thousand volts of pleasure.

"I love how you feel," he whispered gruffly. "So soft. So wet."

Gloria ground herself into his hand. "More," she said.

"Mmm, baby." Dillon twisted his fingers and pulsed them against the walls of her sex, twisting, withdrawing, plunging.

"More, Dillon. Please."

He guided his cock to her soaked opening and then propped himself up on one arm. She gazed through the haze that surrounded her, into Dillon's face, his expression both serious and tender. But when he finally thrust, finally giving her what she wanted, the sensation of his body joining with hers, stretching her and filling her was more than she could take. There was no way she could keep her eyes open.

She cried out as he withdrew, and moaned as he thrust again.

"Dillon!" His name had suddenly become synonymous

with ecstasy and Gloria used it that way, chanting it like a mantra. "Dillon." She sighed. "Dillon. Oh, Dillon…" And then she exploded, losing control in a way she never had with any other man.

"Sweetheart…"

With emotion clogging her throat, she begged, "Don't stop. Please. Don't stop."

Bless the man, he didn't stop. Rather, he increased the pace, settling more of his wonderful weight on her. His chin rested on the top of her head, bringing his corded neck within sucking and biting distance.

"Oh, baby."

She loved the emotion that spoke of his loss of control, making his normally deep, melodic voice harsh and needy.

"Gloria. Oh, baby. I need to."

"Yes." Her fingers bit into him as surely as her teeth had, and Gloria thrust up to meet him just as he drove himself as deep into her as possible, making the very depths of her sing. Two, three, four more short bursts and Dillon howled, holding on to her hip as he quaked inside of her.

Slowly, slowly, Gloria came back to herself as if a part of her had disengaged from her body and floated up to the ceiling, dancing on the roof to the sound of the now-gentle rain.

"You okay?" Dillon rolled them to their sides and stroked her cheek, gazing with concern into her eyes.

"I'm better than okay." She smiled, but Dillon's expression of concern didn't let up. "Dillon, I'm not going to freak."

"You sure?"

God. They'd just had spectacular cabin sex and he was still worried that she was going to go nutty on him.

"I promise." She kissed him, softly at first, but it quickly grew in passion.

"You trying to kill me?" Dillon asked, groaning as he pulled out, leaving a cool emptiness in his wake.

"Oh." Gloria clutched at his hips to no avail. "Don't go."

"One condom. That's all I've got." He smoothed her messy hair out of her face. "And believe me, with that kiss and a little movement in your hips, I'm ready to go all over again."

10

THE WET GROUND was steaming in the morning sun. Dillon had let the horses out of the shed to graze, and now stood by the rain barrel, dipping a pail for fresh water. With pail in hand, he paused outside the door, feeling... what? Cautious?

Yeah. That was what it was. The same kind of feeling he'd always felt when approaching a mare and her new foal for the first time, careful so as not to startle mother or baby. Wanting them to trust him and be comfortable with him.

When he'd gotten up, Gloria had still been sleeping on the floor by the hearth, looking like an angel with a halo of tangled red hair, but when he opened the door, she was up and dressed, her back to him as she went through the cupboards. Who was going to greet him today? The passionate woman from last night? The bossy designer who was cool and efficient? Or, the cold woman who kept her emotions hidden behind a facade of disdain?

But the woman who turned to him was someone he'd never met before. Her face was pale, her eyes were bright, and her smile was...shy. Dammit, if that smile didn't just tug at something low in his belly. Something protective.

"You sleep okay?" Dillon asked, pouring fresh water into the washbasin.

"Mmm-hmm."

"Good."

She glanced up and smiled that smile again.

He moved up to her and slipped his hand lightly around her delicate neck. "We okay?"

She nodded, her eyes going liquid as if she might cry, for shit's sake.

Normally that sort of emotion would scare Dillon off in a big way. But with Red, it made him feel as though his innards were composed of oatmeal. Mush and brown sugar. He bent low, his back not happy with the movement, and kissed her softly. Licking her lips because she tasted like honey.

"I'm glad."

The ride back to the ranch was done slowly and in silence. Now that it was daylight, Dillon was able to get a better idea of the damage caused by the storm. Part of the hill had caved and lots of trees were down, but at least the house and outbuildings hadn't been affected.

A man on a horse approached and as he neared he could make out the ranch hand, Thad.

"Morning," Thad called. "You two hole up at the Doghouse last night?"

"Uh-huh," Dillon said.

"That was smart." Thad's gaze swept from one to the other.

Dillon caught sight of a pretty pink hue sneaking up the back of Red's neck. He tried his best to contain his grin.

Turning his attention to Dillon, Thad asked, "How many did you lose last night?"

"One."

He nodded. "There was a whole group of them that got caught up against the pilings of the washed-out bridge. Four or five maybe. It was hard to tell in that dark."

"That's a shame."

"You said it. Hate to lose a head let alone five." Thad scratched his cheek and then pointed to the house. "Power's still out, but the generator's running. Left some breakfast in the kitchen for the two of you. I'll wager you're starving something fierce."

"I could eat," Dillon said, catching Gloria's eyes. In the morning light, her eyes were like two gems peeping out of her flushed face. Suddenly Dillon had visions of consuming something other than food. Parts of Red's body came to mind. Parts that he'd barely had a chance to explore last night.

Gloria's already pink cheeks deepened in color and she tore her gaze from his. "That's very kind of you, Thaddeus. I appreciate it."

"We'll need your help today, Dill." Thad turned his attention to Gloria, as if asking for permission. As if she was the lady of the house.

Dillon moved up beside Gloria and said to her, "Sorry, but the work on the house is going to have to wait."

"You do what you have to do. I've got plenty to keep me busy." She smiled, a version of that shy smile all over again.

Maneuvering his horse closer to Gloria, Dillon brushed her thigh, gently. "Let's go eat. I'm starving and a hot shower wouldn't hurt, either." He winked and then prodded the horse in the direction of the barn. As the horse's walk turned into a trot, he overheard Gloria clearing her throat and Thad asking her how her sleep in the Doghouse was.

Dillon broke into a smile when he heard her say, "It was wonderful."

AFTER A BREAKFAST of sausage, eggs, hash browns and ham—not a fruit or vegetable to be found—Gloria went to work on the second floor of the ranch house. She felt like the Tasmanian Devil, whirling through the rooms like a human tornado, clearing them of all personal effects. It didn't take long—purging other people's belongings was easy when you had no sentimental value attached to them. Before Dillon had taken off to help Thad and Curtis with ranch work, he'd found loads of boxes and crates that she could use to pack things up. There were always three piles: garbage, donation, keep. The first and second were always the biggest, it was amazing what junk people held on to.

"What's this?" she muttered aloud. One whole side of the closet in the master bedroom was piled with boxes marked "clothes." Opening the top box, she was surprised to find women's clothing—jeans, blouses, dresses—much of it practically brand-new. She pulled a dress from the box and, standing in front of the mirror, held the dress up against herself. It was lemon yellow with ruffles on the bodice and spaghetti straps. She stripped and pulled the sundress over her head and stood in front of the mirror, turning this way and that, checking out her reflection. It fit perfectly after she'd adjusted the straps to her frame. She swiveled her hips and the full skirt swirled out around her legs.

"I love it."

She didn't know why she left it on other than it made her feel pretty, which the yoga clothes definitely didn't do. With a hand to her cheek, she stared at her reflection. She looked…different. It could be that she'd showered and applied a bit of makeup from her purse, but Gloria didn't think that was it because she *felt* different, too. Not panicky, not unsettled, not rushed.

Content.

A panic attack would have been farthest from her mind if not for the careful way Dillon had treated her this morning, as though she was fragile china that needed to be protected by bubble wrap. Even that was strangely nice, being treated with care and concern. When was the last time anyone had treated her that way?

She regarded her reflection, wondering what Dillon would think if he saw her in the dress. Okay, she admitted it. She *wanted* Dillon to see her in it. How would he react? Would he pull her close? Reach up under the skirt and caress her leg? Would he find her wet and willing—yes!—and proceed to explore her most intimate parts?

Damn, calloused fingers felt good on a woman.

In a woman.

Fanning her face, Gloria pulled herself away from the mirror and followed the stairs down to the main level. There was so much work to do still—she had to control her rambling thoughts.

She caught sight of her handbag sitting at the front door and realized she hadn't checked up on her father since she'd arrived. Tucked into the front pocket was her phone, which was nearly dead. She tried calling home but only got a couple of beeps, telling her there was no service.

I'm sure he's fine.

After plugging in her phone to charge, Gloria made her way to the kitchen, doing an impromptu dance step as she went, enjoying the soft cotton swirling around her legs. Passing through the kitchen, she returned to the larder, at least that was what Max Ozark had called it. It was a big room with lots of shelves full of preserves and canned goods that were labeled with dates—over a decade old. There was a metal canister marked "Flour" and all of the necessities for baking: salt, sugar, baking powder, yeast.

Looking around at the large space, she imagined how it

could look, very country kitchen with labeled mason jars, ceramic crockery and brass pots hanging from the rafters. She made a mental note of all the work that needed to be done and then found herself playing with the soft cotton of the skirt she wore.

Maybe it was the dress that was giving Gloria peculiar ideas, because the ingredients in the larder and a basket that sat high on the shelf prompted a plan that had nothing to do with remodeling the room. And everything to do with Dillon.

THE SMELL OF freshly baked something-or-other greeted Dillon as he walked into the ranch house. "Something smells good in here," he called. "What have you been up to…whoa." Dillon took one look at Gloria and removed his hat, an automatic response when in the presence of a lady, something his mother had drilled into him since he was a kid.

"You look…nice." He walked around her, slowly, taking in the yellow sundress, the Western ruffles at the top, the full skirt, the low cut that was flattering to her form and tempting to his fingers. Add to that the spaghetti straps that let him know she wasn't wearing a bra underneath and Dillon was reduced to thinking with only one part of his body. "Where did you get the dress?"

"There was a bunch of women's clothes boxed up in the master bedroom." She held it out by the skirt. "I hope it's okay that I'm wearing it. My stuff is pretty dirty."

Dillon frowned. The dress had belonged to Char. Why the hell had Kenny held on to her stuff after all this time?

"Who did it belong to?"

"Kenny's ex-wife."

"Kenny was married?"

"Uh-huh."

"And she didn't take her clothes?" Gloria indicated her dress.

"She left all of a sudden."

"What about the ranch? Isn't she entitled?" She indicated the house with a sweep of her hand.

"No. It ended a while back. Signed and sealed."

"Ah." Gloria fingered the skirt. "Maybe I should change."

Dillon came closer. "No. Leave it on." His fingers trailed along the bare skin of her shoulders and beneath her hair. "It suits you."

"Thanks," she said, turning her face up as if she was hoping for a kiss, which was exactly what he wanted to do…once he'd cleaned some of the mud and grime off himself.

Instead of a kiss, he asked, "So, what's all this about? You looking so…good." He sniffed. "And is that fresh baking I smell?"

"Yes."

He leaned low and placed a soft kiss on her shoulder, unable to keep away when Gloria's bare skin was within kissing distance. She smelled like shampoo. Clean and sweet.

"I found some ingredients in the larder," she whispered. "I made some buns, at least, they were supposed to be buns."

"For dinner?" For some reason the idea of this woman cooking for him was incredibly intimate and Dillon cupped her jaw in order to tilt her head back and give him access to her tasty neck.

"I thought maybe we could go for a ride."

"A ride?" Was it wrong to feel a surge of testosterone when Gloria willingly gave up her throat to him? He ran his thumb beneath her jaw and gently down the length of her long neck. He stopped kissing when he realized he was leaving dirty streaks on her pristine skin.

She opened her eyes, startled as if she hadn't realized what he'd been doing. Or, what she'd been doing. She cleared her throat. "Yeah. I thought we could go for a—"

"Picnic?"

"Is that okay?"

"Nothing better. Let me go shower first. I'm filthy."

He was downstairs in ten and they were saddled and ready to ride fifteen minutes later. Dillon didn't think about where he was taking her until he was nearly there, the house peeking through the trees up ahead.

"Who lives there?" Gloria asked, pointing at the house that was visible between the trees. When he didn't answer she urged her horse right up beside his. "Dillon?"

Was it the house in the distance or the woman beside him that was distracting him? Probably both. But he couldn't help being distracted. Gloria looked like something out of some damn fairy tale, riding astride, wearing that sexy yellow dress, the sun making her hair look like flames blowing in the soft breeze. She was so relaxed on the back of a horse, and in his estimation, there was nothing sexier than a woman who was comfortable on the back of an animal. Well, maybe he could think of a few things that might be sexier, like said woman lying flat on her back, fiery hair streaming out on the wool blanket beneath her.

"Are you going to answer me or just stare at me?"

"Sorry, Red. Flashbacks."

A switch somewhere beneath her skin flipped and she went pink all over. Sweet as hell.

By the time he paid attention to his surroundings again, they were approaching the abandoned house.

"Are we trespassing?"

"Yes." He adjusted his hat. "But don't worry. No one lives there anymore."

She threw him a questioning glance but he rode past, not willing to explain just yet. Once they got right up to the house, he dismounted, tied his horse to a fence post and stood waiting for Gloria to do the same. Did the fact that he was hoping to catch a glimpse beneath her skirt as she lifted her leg over the horse make him a dirty-minded jackass? Maybe, but he didn't care.

Red dismounted gracefully, however, keeping her good bits hidden. Making him lust for her even more than if he'd caught sight of those lacy panties that didn't seem practical enough to be called underwear.

Once she was standing beside him, he took her hand and led her up the steps to the wraparound porch. The whole thing was looking worn and needed to be refinished, but no one was going to do that because no one cared about this place anymore. Because the people who'd bought the placed cared so little, the key that had always been stashed in the hollow at the top of the door frame was still there.

"Um, isn't this breaking and entering?" Gloria asked, tugging Dillon back before he could open the door.

He glanced down at her. "Nope. Not when you use a key." He held it for her to see.

She stood her ground, frowning.

"Don't worry. No one lives here."

"And who used to live here?"

He smiled. "Me."

11

She let Dillon lead her through the main floor of the large country house. It was one of those places that seemed to have been added to with each generation so that just when she thought she'd seen it all, there was another little addition somewhere.

"Why doesn't anyone live here?" Her designer's eye filled the space with rugs and furniture, changing out the lighting, sweeping out the cobwebs and removing the peeling wallpaper, freshening everything up with a new coat of paint. It could be a great house. Lots of character.

"It wasn't bought by a family but by Technofarm. It's a ranching conglomerate. They set up a camp closer to the road. There's a big stockyard there now."

Dillon released her hand to go stand by a picture window that overlooked a forest with mountains in the background. The view was stunning.

"Such a shame."

"Yep."

With his hat pulled low on his brow, Gloria was left to guess what his expression was, but by the way he gazed out the window, his fists clenched at his sides, his back ramrod straight as if all his muscles were strained, she had a pretty good idea. He was seeing his family here. Could probably still feel their presence because Gloria could, too.

"Why'd you sell?"

Still gazing out the window, Dillon said, "Long story."

She wanted to ask about it but something told her that Dillon would tell her in his own time, when he was ready. So, she went to stand beside him and she imagined what life would have been like growing up here. Land that belonged to you as far as the eye could see. Wildlife, the fresh scent of the outdoors combined with the aromas of home-cooked meals. Gloria knew what that smelled like, her best friend owned a bakery and there was nothing like the warm scent of fresh baking to make a place smell like home, which was why Realtors baked cookies when they showed a house. People walked in and already felt like they were at home.

As she gazed out the window, she heard the ghost of kids' voices. Yelling and playing. Running around. No junk to impede their movement, no sound of nearby traffic. Fresh air instead of the stench of rotting garbage.

"Do you have any brothers and sisters?" she asked, casting a sideways glance up at the man by her side.

"Two brothers. One older, one younger."

"What are their names?"

"Colton's the baby. Five years younger than me."

"And the older one?"

"His name was Carson." That was it. No other explanation. But his use of the past tense did not go unnoticed.

Eventually he turned to her. "You want to see upstairs?"

She nodded.

Dillon led the way up the narrow stairs to the second floor, and Gloria asked, "How old is this house?"

"The original was built in the twenties. It's expanded over the years."

"It's a shame to just leave it empty."

"Yep. They should probably bulldoze it but it costs too much. It'll just stay here until it eventually falls down." He spoke without any inflection, as if he wasn't talking about his family home. She understood that.

He stopped inside the doorway of a small bedroom, and stood motionless for a moment. When he turned and flashed a smile, Gloria wondered how genuine it was. "You are about to see something very few women have ever seen."

"Your bedroom?"

"Uh-huh."

While he stayed at the door, she entered the room and went to stand at the window. Much like downstairs, the view was spectacular.

"When I was a teenager, I'd climb out that window nearly every night."

She turned, picturing a young Dillon. "What would you do? Where would you go?"

"Sometimes Kenny and I would meet up to sneak smokes and whiskey. God. We thought we were so grown up." He rubbed his chin with the heel of his hand. "Sometimes we'd spy on the poker games over at the Doghouse. When we were sixteen, the men caught us, but instead of sending us home, they let us join. That was a rite of passage, I tell you."

"What about your older brother? Did he play, too?"

"Nah. Carson was ten years older than me. He was a man when I was just a kid." He chuckled. "I used to think my parents were nuts for having us so far apart, though I doubt it was on purpose. We just showed up when we did."

"Where is everyone now?"

"Well, my brother Carson was killed in the service. Afghanistan. After he died, things went sideways and my parents sold and moved down to Yuma. Colton moved with them but returned every summer, working on Kenny's ranch as a hand. Dad died of a stroke a couple years later and Mom just decided to stay down South."

"Oh, Dillon. I'm sorry. Losing a brother and your father. That must have been rough."

Dillon's gaze roamed the room as if he was seeing something that wasn't there. Finally he said, "Let's get out of here."

There was nothing Gloria wanted more than to continue to explore the abandoned house where Dillon had grown up, but by the look on his face, the memories were too much.

Once back on the porch, Gloria said, "Thanks for bringing me here."

He gave a one-shoulder shrug as if to say it was nothing. But if it was nothing, why was his jaw so tense, creating a hollow in his wide cheeks? Why did he keep opening and closing his hands into fists and why couldn't he meet her gaze?

Which begged the question, why had he brought her here in the first place?

"WHAT DO YOU THINK?"

They emerged from a single track path through the woods into a meadow filled with natural grass and wildflowers, a bunch of bright yellows and reds belonging to plants that Gloria was unfamiliar with.

"It's beautiful." She gazed around. A small crystal clear lake was at the center of the meadow. "And this was your backyard?" She smiled. "How terrible it must have been."

"It's not bad."

Not bad? If he only knew. When her mom was alive, their backyard had been filled with flowers and quirky garden sculptures. Gnomes and birdbaths and little signs and whatnots. Cluttered but usable. In the years that followed, the outdoor space was filled with junk, and then more junk. It was claustrophobic and the only time she'd felt as if she could breathe was when she was sent away to camp.

After tramping down a section of grass, Dillon spread an old patchwork quilt on the ground and together they unloaded the contents of the basket: jam from 2005— she hoped it was still good—pickles from about the same era. Leftover sausages from breakfast and the buns she'd baked that looked more like pancakes because the yeast must have been too old.

"I know it's not much. And if you don't eat the buns, you won't hurt my feelings."

"It's fine. Better than fine."

She reached inside the basket and withdrew the iced tea she'd made and poured it into two plastic cups. "We keep this diet up and we're going to get scurvy."

He laughed. "Don't worry. We'll go to town for supplies in the next day or two."

"Will the bridge be fixed?"

"Nah. Probably won't be until sometime this summer. We'll wait for the water level to recede some more and then there's a place I can cross with my truck. Just need the mud to dry a little more."

"Oh." The thought of returning to her tiny hotel room in Half Moon Creek took some of the zest out of her.

"You won't be able to drive the car back, though. Even if it is fixed. You'll have to ride with me, every day."

Gloria kept her gaze down in order to hide her smile. Why the thought of driving to and from the ranch with Dillon every day made her smile...

Really, genius? Maybe because you like him. Duh.

Snarky conscience.

Yes, she liked him. Probably too much. In fact she was going to have to be careful because this job would be done and over before she knew it.

You could always stretch it out. There's plenty of work to be done. Maybe see if there's other work in the area...

Gloria quieted the voice in her head by filling paper plates for herself and Dillon. It was a habit that she'd formed living alone with her dad. He was always so preoccupied with everything, he often forgot to eat.

"So," she asked, "how long have you been riding bulls?"

"Since I was sixteen." Dillon put a hand to his lower back, as though the thought of his profession made his back ache. "But professionally? Since I was nineteen."

"And, you can make a living, doing it?"

"Yep. You've got to follow the circuit, rodeo after rodeo. But, you can make big money. If you win."

"So? Do you win?" Gloria gazed up at him through her lashes, a coy gesture, she realized. But there was something about sitting on a blanket, wearing a dress, having a picnic with this stoic, proud man, that made her feel as if she and Dillon had been whisked back in time and were courting, old-fashioned-style.

As if they hadn't just had wonderful stuck-in-a-cabin-so-let's-do-it sex last night and wild, tipsy my-best-friend-just-got-married-so-let's-do-it sex three months ago. Though parts of her body were continually reliving those moments—in vivid detail—throbbing and pulsing in blissful remembrance, her emotions were somewhat more chaste.

"You should come watch sometime."

"Huh?" Gloria gave her head a shake, bringing her back to the present day.

"The county fair and rodeo is coming up. You should come watch."

"I'd like that."

"What about you? What made you decide to go into interior design and staging?"

She should have known that the conversation would turn to her, so why did she feel so unprepared to answer? Maybe because Dillon had shared so much of himself today—taking her to his old house, showing her his room, telling her about his brother's and father's deaths, though there was more said in body language and subtext than in actual words.

A part of her wanted to open up to him, to tell him the truth about what happened after her mom died, but Gloria couldn't bring herself to do it. Tugging on a loose thread on the quilt, she said, "I like things orderly. I know it's weird, but it makes me feel good to organize things."

"Yeah, I can see that about you."

She glanced up. "So, why'd you give me such a hard time at the fund-raiser last year?"

A playful glint came into his eyes. "What do you mean?"

"Come on. You purposefully undid everything I tried to do, from banner placement to balloon arrangements to just generally getting in my way."

"You really don't know why?"

"Because you're a macho jerk?" She'd said nearly the very same thing over a year ago when the man had annoyed the hell out of her. Now the words carried no conviction whatsoever.

"I was just trying to get your attention, Red."

"Well, you certainly did that." She nudged him with her body. God, the man was a wall.

A serious expression came over him. "I liked you from the start. Something about you." He touched her cheek.

The caress was so gentle and sincere, it took Gloria's breath away.

"That night in Chicago...?" He tilted her face to meet his gaze. "It *wasn't* a mistake. Not for me."

Was it the angle of her head that made her throat feel constricted?

"Then, last night? Well, I sure as hell hope you don't think that was a mistake."

Gloria meant to shake her head, but Dillon had a grasp on her chin and he held her in place as he leaned toward her and whispered, "Because I don't."

Before he kissed her, Gloria reached out and removed his hat. There, now she could see his face. "I don't think it was a mistake, either."

"Good." He ran a hand through his hair, a mischievous grin playing at the corners of his mouth. He reached into his pocket and pulled out a plastic square. "Because I'm planning on making it happen all over again."

"Where'd you find that?"

"Thad gave it to me. Must have recognized the guilty expressions on our faces this morning."

"Oh, God."

"He's quite the ladies' man, our Thaddeus."

"Stop." She covered her face, laughing with a twinge of discomfort as she imagined the cowboy thinking about what the two of them had been up to last night. Dillon pried her fingers away from her face in order to place the plastic square in her hand. "I'll just leave that right there." He closed her hand around it. "Now it's up to you."

He nudged one of the thin straps of her dress, making it slide down her arm and kissed the top of her shoulder.

"Why are you leaving it up to me?"

"Because." His fingers traced along the top of the bodice, grazing her until her skin sang with yearning.

"It should be a joint decision."

He tasted the inside of her ear and nibbled her lobe, whispering, "Babe, I'm telling you what I want…" His hand covered her breast and gently squeezed. "Right this second."

"Presumptuous cowboy."

"Sexy city girl." He held the back of her head, angling her in order to gently lick the side of her neck. "I love your neck, have I mentioned?"

"Mmm."

The kisses continued, soft and sweet, leaving Gloria boneless as she leaned against the mountain-of-a-man beside her. When the second strap fell away, she moaned, "What are you doing?"

"What do you think?" He tugged on the zipper at the back of her dress. "You took off my hat, only fair I disrobe you."

She clutched at the front of her dress because she wasn't wearing a bra underneath. "I hardly think that's fair." She searched the surrounding area. "Plus, we're in public."

Dillon leaned in and placed a soft, iced tea–flavored kiss on her lips. "Darlin' there isn't another soul for miles around. Don't tell me you've never made love in the out of doors?"

"Well…"

"Oh, honey, you don't know what you're missing."

Gripping the front of her dress, she whispered, "But… here?"

"Damn straight."

"But—"

Those naughty fingers of his found the zipper again and tugged all the way down. "Trust me."

She leaned closer, keeping her dress up with one hand

while touching his jaw with the other. God, she loved the man's face. "Okay. I trust you."

"Good." He pulled her hands away from her chest, allowing the top of it to slide down, revealing her bare skin. Dillon's groan of appreciation was enough to make her forget she was now topless in public.

"It's like you're not real." He drew a finger down between her breasts, circling one and then the other before cupping her in his big hand. "You're like a mythical creature—a mermaid or a wood nymph." He ran a thumb across her nipple. "Or maybe a fairy queen."

It was a whimsical notion, not something she expected from Dillon, but when he latched on to her nipple and sucked, Gloria gave herself over to the divine sensation. Throwing her head back, she gazed through hooded lids up at the wide expanse of incredibly blue sky. Maybe she was caught up in a fairy tale, maybe none of this was real, because this moment, this experience, was so far outside the realm of her day-to-day life, it felt magical, dreamlike.

Dillon blindly swept the empty plates and food containers to the side and eased her back onto the quilt, lying beside her, giving him the opportunity to both have his way with her and watch what he was doing. From the intensity of his gaze, he seemed to like the look of his tanned hand against her pale skin. Gloria sure did.

"That feels so good," Gloria said, as he brushed a thumb back and forth across her nipple.

"For you and me both."

She arched her back, pressing herself into his hand, an automatic response to the tantalizing sensation of his touch.

"Woman." He leaned over and took more than just her nipple in his mouth, as though he was ravenous and she evoked an unquenchable hunger. Up until now, he'd been

so gentle—last night, this morning. But now? Now he was
letting loose and Gloria loved it. The scratch of his short
beard against her sensitive skin, the suction of his warm
mouth, the roughness of his hand.

"Dillon." She loved his name. It was more than a name,
it was synonymous with *pleasure*.

As he moved from beside her to on top of her, Gloria
frantically worked the buttons on his shirt, needing to
touch him. What a wonder it would be to see such a magnificent man in the full light of day! Somehow she managed to fumble through all the buttons and tug the shirt
from his jeans.

"Oh, baby," he said, moaning hoarsely in her ear. "Your
touch drives me wild."

"So does yours." She tried to undo his belt but there was
a big buckle in the way and she didn't know how to work it.

"Dillon?"

He didn't answer. He was too busy using his mouth to
make love to her breasts while searching up underneath
her skirt with his free hand. Gloria forgot about his belt
buckle because Dillon's hand kept climbing the inside of
her thigh and she realized he was about to discover that
she had a secret.

12

HIS FINGERS STILLED when he reached the very top of her thigh. He propped himself up on his elbow and stared down at her with wonder and wicked surprise. "No panties, Red?"

She shook her head. After showering, she'd washed her underwear in the sink and they were still hanging to dry.

He let out a low growl and then propped himself up higher. Taking the hem of her skirt, he slowly pushed it up her legs, never taking his gaze from what he was doing. The cool cotton slithered up past her knees and higher and Dillon didn't stop until the skirt was bunched up around her waist and she was completely exposed to the elements.

It was marvelous.

She should have felt embarrassed. She didn't. Gloria felt beautiful and powerful. Maybe it had something to do with the rapt expression that Dillon wore as he gazed down at her, as if he was completely and utterly under her spell.

"Dillon?"

"Yeah, baby?" He touched her, stroking her mound before easing two fingers between her folds and dipping inside. His groan told her how wet she was, how ready. Not that she needed proof, she already knew what she wanted.

Him. Though the way he plunged two fingers deep, almost made her forget what she was going to ask until he leaned closer, and Gloria felt the bite of his buckle on her hip.

"Take off your belt," she whispered.

"Hmm?"

"Your belt. Please."

He had to pull his hand from her in order to do as she asked and Gloria immediately missed his touch. But once his belt was loosened, she got to work on his fly—buttons, nice—giving her room to fit her hand inside. How on earth could he stand being cooped up behind that fly? He was so wonderfully aroused, she had to free him of his shorts, needed to touch him.

"Oh, baby," he groaned. "I love that." He dipped his face to hers and kissed her, filling the inside of her mouth with his talented tongue, sucking on her lips as she squeezed his length, up and down, marveling at how he continued to grow in her grasp.

"Where's the condom?" His voice was hoarse.

She found it where she'd left it, beside her hip, and handed it to him.

"I said it was up to you, but…"

"Put it on. Now."

His eyes rolled back in relief and Dillon pushed himself to his knees so he could roll the rubber over his length. It was a magnificent sight with the sun shining behind him, the sound of the bees, a dragonfly hovering for a moment before taking off. It should have seemed improper to be doing what they were doing, but the truth was, it felt anything but.

It felt right.

Once finished, Dillon reached for her knees, grasped and tugged her toward him, spreading her before him. "I'm sorry but," he groaned as he slid his hands down her thighs and impaled her with both thumbs, "I need you, right now." He stroked inside of her and then massaged her clit, back and forth, round and round. "Is that okay?"

"Hell, yes."

Guiding himself to her entrance, he stayed there for a second before shifting his weight forward and filling her in one sure stroke.

Oh! How could something feel so good? How was it possible to feel as if her body was made just for this? To have this man fill her and complete her and move inside of her as though there was no other place he should be but right where he was, right now?

She worked her hands into his open shirt and gripped his powerful shoulders, urging him on by raising her hips to meet each and every wonderful thrust.

She fought the urge to shut her eyes, because part of the pleasure came from watching and seeing her surroundings. Experiencing this, as if this was the first time she'd ever had sex. Marveling in the beautiful expression of concentration on Dillon's face as if making love to her was the most important job in the world. Seeing his features change as he increased his pace, bringing himself nearer to climax.

Just the thought of him, releasing inside of her, pushed her over the edge, and Gloria tilted her chin to the sky, crying out in ecstasy. Joining her voice with the buzz of the bees and the wind and the trickle of the creek flowing into the pond, as if she was one with not only Dillon, but with this place.

"Oh, babe." His fingers dug into her hips as he filled her one last time, and she felt his orgasm pound up from the very base of him and along his length in powerful pulses.

One thought consumed her.

I want this again.

DILLON ROLLED OVER in the big bed. Unlike the morning after the wedding, when he went to reach for Gloria, she was there, her warm, naked body nestled perfectly in the circle of his arms. Sleepy, contented sounds came out of her as though she was a kitten curled up in the sun, purring. It was the third morning in a row he'd woken up to her, if you counted the cabin. Which he most certainly did.

Damn. He could get used to this.

Working hard all day, cooking up a meal from scratch, lighting a fire and reading or playing cribbage, a game both of them knew. Making bets as to who would win, bets involving taking off articles of clothes and such.

Showering together. Making love together. Over and over again. Even when he thought he was done, all she had to do was nestle her sweet little ass against him and he was ready to go one more time.

Making love to Gloria was a new experience for him: fun, erotic, but something else, too. There were tender times and passionate times that went beyond any sexual encounter he'd had before and while he lay in bed, Dillon could practically see the two of them working the ranch together, as if *this* was where she belonged. In Montana. With him.

She rolled in his arms and pressed a sleepy kiss on his chest.

That kiss might as well have been a hot coal because it spread flames out in every direction, waking up his senses and another part of him that was incredibly attuned to every movement of her body.

He wanted nothing more than to make love to her again this morning. And again tomorrow morning.

Dillon stroked the tangled curls at the top of her head and held her close.

As much as he was enjoying himself—the word *enjoy*

didn't actually do justice to how he felt—he had to remind himself that Gloria did *not* belong here. Didn't matter that she could ride with the best of them and that she seemed content and relaxed. Her life was in Chicago and he needed to curb all these warm, tender thoughts right here and now.

Except that Gloria was drowsily caressing his thigh which was *not* conducive to curbing sensual, tender thoughts in the least. Her actions were producing thoughts of the lustful variety. Thoughts that involved spreading her thighs and filling her until she cried out his name, for example.

Dillon rolled over and sat up.

"Where are you going?" she asked as he strode naked from the room.

"Shower." The only way to curb his arousal right now was a little distance and a nice cold shower.

GLORIA UNDERSTOOD WHY a 4x4 vehicle was necessary when living on a ranch. Not only had the bridge been washed out, but parts of the road, too. The forty-minute drive to town took them an hour, not that Gloria minded. She spent the entire trip thinking about the past few days. The cabin, the ride, the picnic. Working together in the house. She'd had to measure each room for her 3-D software and Dillon had helped, though it took longer when he kept interrupting the process with kisses and hot-and-heavy grope sessions.

She smiled to herself in remembrance. When was the last time she'd had so much fun?

Then there were the evenings spent together in the great room in front of the fire. No TV, no internet. No cell service. Nothing but each other. Out of habit, she worked, while he read whatever he could lay his hands on—biographies, historic novels, the farmer's almanac—the man was a voracious reader. Then the games began. Strip crib-bage? She'd never heard of it.

So fun.

And, it all seemed so natural. From the stormy night in the cabin, to making love outside, to falling into bed together back at the ranch. Gloria still couldn't believe she'd done all that, particularly the outdoor sex thing. God! Her friends would never believe it in a million years. She wouldn't have believed it about herself, except that she was there, she'd done it. And the event continued to play on a loop in her brain, not allowing her to forget.

Not that she wanted to forget.

The only downside was that Dillon had seemed a little distant this morning. But then, he'd gotten up early and taken off to help with chores. It was probably all in her imagination. Even if it wasn't, they were going back to town, to separate places. Would things change? Would their relationship go back to strictly business?

As Dillon drove down the main street of Half Moon Creek, her phone suddenly started beeping from the depths of her purse. She fished it out and held it up. "I've got a signal again."

"Welcome back to civilization."

Before she had a chance to go through her messages, they'd pulled up in front of the Gold Dust Hotel.

Not one word had been said about where they went from here. Maybe it was understood from his side of things, but it certainly wasn't from hers. She had no idea where she stood with him and she had a sudden need to ask. Yet, for some reason, Gloria was experiencing difficulty bringing it up. When Dillon came around to her side of the truck in order to open the door for her—she loved that he did that, though it was completely unnecessary—she figured it was her last chance to say something.

But Dillon beat her to it. "I'll pick you up tomorrow at five thirty."

She choked. "In the morning?"

"Yep. Work starts early on a ranch. Those boys have more work right now than they can manage."

"Oh." Gloria frowned. "Why don't…" she paused "…you just stay out there? Wouldn't that make life easier?" God, she'd just about said, "we—why don't we stay out there?"

"The place isn't mine."

That didn't make sense. The place belonged to Dillon and he worked it as though it belonged to him. The past couple of days had sure made her think of the ranch as his.

Ours.

The word spoken so clearly inside her head startled her, and she realized he was waiting for her to take his hand and step down, so she did. He released her hand the moment she was on the sidewalk.

What was that about? Could be nothing. She was probably being oversensitive. Things were confusing at the moment. Besides, just because they'd slept together, more than once, that didn't make her his girlfriend, and while they hadn't had *the conversation* about where they stood, she could only assume one thing.

It was a one-time thing.

Or a *nine-time* thing. Ten, if you counted Chicago.

"So, we'll see you bright and early, okay?"

Gloria frowned. "Sure."

He leaned low and kissed her cheek, a chaste, brotherly sort of kiss, before rounding the truck and climbing aboard. Nothing more. No offer of dinner, no mention of what had happened between them. Nothing.

"Okay, then. Bye," Gloria said, even though it was pointless because the truck was already pulling away. She watched Dillon's truck drive down the street and then turn the corner a few blocks away.

I am not hurt. I am not upset. This is the way it has to go.

The woman who'd tended bar the other night was behind the counter when Gloria entered the lobby and called to her before she could climb the stairs to her room on the second floor.

"You've got a bunch of messages." In her hand was a stack of notepapers. "Oh, and Walt called. He says your car's fixed."

"Thanks," Gloria said as she walked over, a sense of foreboding filling her because of the sheer number of messages in the woman's hand. Leaning against the counter, she flipped through them. There were two from Daisy and six from Faith.

Shit.

Gloria typed in her password for her phone to find seventeen messages and a bunch of missed calls. Without bothering to read them, Gloria phoned her best friend. Daisy picked up after the second ring.

"Glo? Oh, my God. Where have you been?"

"There was a bad storm here. No service. What's going on?"

"It's your dad. He had a heart attack."

13

THE TRIP HOME was a blur, from throwing things into her bag, to picking up the car and racing off to Butte in order to catch the first flight home. Her dad was in the hospital, fighting for his life, while she'd been living a fantasy— going on picnics and having sex and thinking about happiness and forgetting about her life in Chicago as if it didn't exist.

That was a mistake.

When she landed at O'Hare, Faith was there to pick her up. "Don't panic" were the first words out of her mouth as she gave Gloria a bear hug at the arrival gate. "He's okay. They just kept him a couple days for observation."

There were no tears for Gloria; she needed to be strong and to make up for not being there when her father needed her. It was a forty-five-minute drive to the hospital and Faith tried to fill the silence with questions about Montana but after a number of one-word answers, Gloria finally said, "I quit. That's all you need to know."

"Didn't they understand?"

She shook her head, realizing Faith didn't know Dillon was behind the contract. How could so much have happened in such a short amount of time?

Well, it didn't matter. None of it mattered. She was home now, where she belonged, and there was no point rehashing the whole Montana thing.

When they arrived at Mount Sinai hospital, Faith led her up to the third floor of the cardiac unit and Gloria heard her father's voice from down the hall, upset and agitated. As she neared, she was able to make out the specific complaints.

"I've got too much to do to be sitting here in this bed. Who's in charge? Where's my doctor? Where are my things?"

She stood for a millisecond outside his door, composing herself before entering. "Hi, Dad."

"Gloria?" Gloria's father looked pale and fragile in his hospital gown. His hair was unwashed and in disarray, his eyes watery and bloodshot behind his glasses. "What are you doing here?"

"What do you think I'm doing here? I came to see you." She walked to the bed and sat down on the edge. "How are you?"

"I'm frustrated, that's how I am. They're keeping me here against my will." There was a tube running through his nose and an IV attached to his hand.

Upon seeing her, the nurse gave her a pained expression and said, "Doctor Webber will be with you in a few minutes."

"Thank you." She took her father's hand. "Dad. You're too worked up. You need to rest."

His eyes grew larger behind the glasses. "No, Gloria-Rose. Don't you see? This is all a conspiracy to get me out of my house. For good." He leaned closer and whispered, "I think there was something—a powder maybe—in one of the letters I got from the state department. I opened it and then, *boom!* I couldn't breathe." He leaned even closer and whispered hoarsely, "It was deliberate."

Oh, dear God. Things were worse than she'd thought, and the only way to console her father during moments of acute paranoia was to agree with him. "Okay, Dad. Let me look into it, all right? I'll get everything checked, send the letter off to a lab, if I have to."

"You'll do that?" His gaze was sadly hopeful.

"Of course." She patted his hand, feeling a weight descend upon her shoulders, crushing her.

A couple of minutes later, a very young doctor appeared in the doorway. "Are you Mr. Hurst's daughter?"

"Yes." Gloria got up to shake his hand.

"May I speak to you in the hall?"

Her automatic assumption was that it was dire, and she squeezed her father's hand while pulling in a shaky breath. He held on and whispered, "Don't believe a word he says."

The doctor closed the door after them and said, "Your father had a very mild heart attack. There doesn't seem to be any permanent damage to his heart."

"Oh, thank God."

"But that doesn't mean this wasn't serious. I've given medication to lower his blood pressure, but he needs rest and to be in a low-stress environment. We're releasing him on the condition that he has somewhere to go, somewhere stress free."

Nodding and feeling like another ton of concrete was poured on top of her, Gloria said, "Yes. He'll come home with me. I'll take care of him."

He handed her a few pamphlets. "He needs to be on a low fat, low salt, low sugar diet. No more than thirty minutes of low-impact exercise a day. Walking is good."

"Okay."

"Good. I'll prescribe some anticoagulants and angiotensin receptor blockers to keep his blood pressure from rising. I'll also prescribe some stress meds."

"He won't take them." Gloria sighed. "He won't take any of this. He doesn't take medication."

"He needs to." The doctor scribbled on his pad and then ripped the page off and handed the prescription to her. Before he left, he patted her shoulder, as if he knew what she was in for and was wishing her luck.

Taking another second outside the hospital room door, Gloria plastered on a fake smile and strode back into the room. "Good news, Dad. They're releasing you and I'm going to take you home."

The look of relief on her father's face broke Gloria's heart because the hard truth was, taking her dad back home was not a relief and as much as she wanted to be a good daughter, it felt a whole hell of a lot more like a prison sentence.

DILLON SAT IN his truck outside the Gold Dust for ten minutes before taking his cell phone from the glove compartment and scrolling through his contacts to find Gloria's name. He ran a thumb over the words, a strange action, he realized, as though touching the letters would bring him closer to her. He should have asked her out for dinner or invited her over yesterday. His trailer was a far cry from the ranch house, but surely a woman who was comfortable at the Doghouse wouldn't mind his deluxe trailer. But he was trying to do the gallant thing—though it was nearly killing him—and give her space to make sure she wanted all these wild and wonderful things they were doing.

Okay, that was a lie. He had to figure shit out for himself, too. He wanted Red, like he'd never wanted another. Maybe even more than Char, although the comparison didn't seem equal because the two women were so different. Nothing had brought that home like seeing Gloria in Char's clothes. That had been weird.

He touched the number and put the phone to his ear. After three rings, a sleepy voice answered, "Hello?"

"Did I wake you up?"

"Who is this?"

He chuckled. She was sure out of it in the mornings. "This is your ride. Get up, sleepy bones, it's time to go to work."

There was a pause, followed by a rustling sound. "Dillon?"

"Who else?"

"Oh, God. I totally forgot."

"Wow. You sleep hard." An image of Gloria sleeping nestled in his arms on the floor of the cabin came to mind. He wanted to repeat that before she left. "Okay, Red. I'll give you ten minutes to get your butt down here. Otherwise I'm coming up there, and it won't be pretty."

She sighed heavily into the mouthpiece. "Dillon, I'm not at the hotel."

"What?" He rubbed his jaw. "Where are you?"

"I had to come home. Something happened and—"

"When are you coming back?"

It took her a moment to reply. "I'm not coming back."

"But—"

"Look, I'm sorry, Dillon. I just can't." He heard her take a shuddering breath. "I can't come back. You need to find someone else."

The line went dead before he could ask another question.

What the fuck just happened?

He'd just dropped her off yesterday at noon and today she was back in Chicago? Was it something he'd done? Did she have another one of her attacks?

He slammed his hands against the steering wheel twice before wrenching the truck into gear and driving off. Was this how things went in the big city, hot one minute, cold the next? Did she expect him to pursue her?

Well, if she thought Dillon Cross was going to up and chase her across the country just to be spurned again, she could just keep on dreaming because it wasn't going to happen.

He might seduce, but he never chased.

By the time he arrived at the ranch, he was in a foul mood. Black as the storm clouds that had pummeled the area only four days ago. He sat in his truck for a few minutes, staring at the house but not really seeing it. Finally he got out, slammed the door and gave the wheel a good hard kick.

Not even the courtesy of a phone call? She just left?

He didn't need that kind of drama in his life. Nope.

Good riddance to her. She belonged in Chicago and he was kidding himself if he thought she'd ever belong in a place like this with a guy like him. And what the hell was he doing thinking those thoughts anyway? He wasn't keeping the ranch, so what was the point?

Curtis waved to him from the barn and Dillon acknowledged him with an upward motion of his head. He took his time making his way over to the barn and when he got there, helped Curtis fill the feed troughs with oats and water, appreciating the man's silent ways.

Curtis filled the last of the troughs and then craned his head toward the open barn door. "Where's Chicago?"

"She left." Dillon turned and scratched the nearest horse between the ears.

"She coming back?"

"Nope."

When Curtis didn't say anything more, Dillon glanced over at him. "What?"

"Nothing. Just…it's too bad. I liked her."

"Yeah, well…" Dillon gripped the stall's gate. Hard. He'd already spent too much time thinking about how he liked Gloria. Now he needed something to distract him. "Let's try to clear some of the downed trees and get the cattle back over to graze on the west side."

"Sure thing, boss."

"Don't call me boss."

"Whatever you say."

WHAT WAS THAT NOISE? A bell? A chime? What? Gloria rolled over in bed and reached for her phone. Three thirty in the morning. Ugh.

Flipping the covers off, she got out of bed, threw her housecoat over her silk pajamas and quietly padded down the hall to the kitchen. Her father was there, an ancient typewriter on the table, typing what was no doubt a letter of complaint, and the typewriter dinged every time it came to the edge of the sheet.

She leaned against the wall and watched for a moment. After a week and a half of caring for her father—which was impossible because he wouldn't listen to her, wouldn't take his medications, wouldn't sleep, barely ate—Gloria was exhausted. She was also worried because this past week had forced her to realize just how sick her father was. She supposed she'd always known things were bad; for heaven's sake, the hoarding was a billboard for OCD behavior. But she'd always hoped things were going to get better. Everything was *not* fine and Gloria had no idea what to do about it, leaving her feeling powerless and utterly afraid.

"What are you doing, Dad?" she asked as she entered the room.

He looked up and frowned. "I'm writing letters."

"I can see that." Letter writing was his new obsession. They piled up as surely as he'd piled up magazines and broken flamingos and plant pots and whatever else he'd become obsessed with. At least the letters didn't accumulate because he actually sent them off.

Those poor people on the receiving end of her father's missives.

"It's the middle of the night, Dad."

"Gloria-Rose, these letters won't write themselves."

She came closer, resting her hands on her father's shoulders. "I know, but you need to sleep."

"Plenty of time to sleep when I'm dead."

It was an offhand comment meant in jest, but the immediate thoughts Gloria experienced ranged from panic—because her dad seemed to have a death wish, and she didn't want him to die—to helplessness—because there was nothing she could do for him. Then there was a third thought, the worst one of them all.

A voice from the deepest, darkest part of her wished for what he suggested, to see her father's obsessive life come to an end.

How can you think that?

Rubbing her temples in a guilt-ridden attempt to remove the terrible thoughts, she asked, "Where'd you get the typewriter?" The machine had to be circa 1975.

"That shop down at the end of the street. They were practically giving it away."

Of course they were because it was trash. "I told you, you can use my computer whenever you like."

He shook his head, his eyes wide. "That's how they track you. Everything you do, everything you search, it's all tracked by the *State*." He patted the heavy, metal type-writer. "No, this is the best way."

The machine dinged again and Gloria sighed. "I'm going back to bed, Dad. You should, too."

"When I'm done."

"Okay." Except Gloria knew that he wouldn't.

The rest of the night was spent in fitful sleep, her bizarre dreams filled with bells as she made her way through a maze made up of piles of papers, giant letters and heaps of old typewriters. Every time the bell sounded, she needed to change directions, taking her deeper and deeper into chaos.

Once she got to work, she made an extra strong pot of coffee and sat at her desk, staring blankly at the 3-D pro-file Faith had done for one of their current clients. What she needed to do was itemize the furniture that needed to be leased for the showing, not stare blankly, doing nothing. However for perhaps the first time in her career, Gloria could not bring herself to care about her work.

Finally, after a half hour of blinking and thinking, Glo-ria made a list. Call suppliers. Order paint. Arrange for movers and storage unit. Confirm times with the client. Contact real estate agent and coordinate showings.

All that staring had dried out her eyes, making each blink feel like sandpaper scraping the surface. After find-ing eyedrops in her desk, she tilted her head back to apply them when Faith knocked on her door. She blotted the tears that formed and waited until she could focus, and found Faith standing inside her office, wearing a dopey grin.

"There's someone here to see you."

"Who?"

"Someone." The word was emphasized with an eye-brow wiggle.

"Okay, I'll be right out."

She picked up her mug of coffee and went to the door.

In the reception area was a man who looked too large for the small space. Not only that, he looked completely out of place with his denim jeans, his button-down shirt, his boots and hat.

"Is this the *stupid* cowboy from Wyoming?" Faith whispered but Gloria ignored her because she had tunnel vision and Dillon filled it. Completely.

"Hi, Gloria."

When she finally found her voice, Gloria said, "What the hell are you doing here?"

"I need to talk to you." His gaze flicked to Faith. "Privately."

Oh, no. No. She couldn't see him alone. She was weak where the man was concerned and she couldn't be weak at a time like this. She needed to be strong. In fact, she'd purposefully refrained from telling Dillon about her father because knowing Dillon, he'd show up here—like he was now—trying to take care of things, when there was nothing he could do.

Lifting her chin and pulling her shoulders back, Gloria said, "There's nothing to talk about. I've made my decision, Dillon. If I owe you money, let me know and I'll reimburse you."

He removed his hat. Oh, that wasn't fair because now she could see his wonderful whiskey-colored eyes. "Here's the thing, Red. I need you."

Those three words buckled her knees and Gloria had to hold on to the back of a chair for support.

"I mean, I can do all those repairs you mentioned. But I haven't the first clue about how to arrange the house or do any of that shit."

"You don't need me," she said. "You could ask Sage from the shop to help you. She's got a good eye. Or Faith, my assistant, could go."

"I could," Faith piped up.

His nostrils flared as if he'd taken a deep breath. "I don't want Sage...or Faith. No offense." He directed this last part toward the young woman.

"None taken."

He swept his gaze over to Gloria. "I want you."

Three more words that nearly killed her. "Look, Dillon. I'm sorry. A personal issue has come up and I..."

All of a sudden, everything that she was trying to do was too much. The sleepless nights, the worry over her father, the loss of the big contract, the empty bank account. The letters. The letters would never end.

Out of nowhere, Gloria felt the world crashing in around her. The walls compressing her. The weight she carried, crushing her. And the man she *least* wanted to break down in front of, stood directly in front of her.

No.

"Leave Dillon," she managed to choke out. "You need to leave right now." She would *not* let him see her this way. He could never see her this way again.

She turned and went back to her office, closing her door firmly and falling against it.

14

THERE WAS ONLY one place to go when he felt like this.

His cousins' private boxing club.

Dillon needed to beat the shit out of someone.

He parked his rental truck a block away and found himself standing on the step outside of the large double doors, waiting for someone to open up. One of the former profootball players opened the door, Owen something-or-other and the two recognized each other from Dillon's previous visit.

The place was exactly as he remembered it, workout stations—large bags, speed bags, weight benches, free weights, surrounding the center ring where two guys were currently fighting. One of the guys was Jamie, his cousin. Or, was that his twin brother, Colin? Hard to tell from this distance.

"Come on, Jamie!" A feminine voice hollered from ringside. "Elbows in. You're broadcasting."

Dillon went to stand beside Jamie's wife to watch the fight. At first she didn't notice his presence, maybe because she was so enthralled in what was going on in the ring, but then she peeked up at him, her eyes widening when she realized who he was. Daisy threw her arms around him. "Dillon! So good to see you."

They went back to watching the fight, though she had a million questions for him in quick staccato.

"How's the ranch. Have you sold it? What are you doing here? Have you spoken to Gloria?"

"Tried. She won't talk to me."

"She's not talking to many people."

"Yeah. I'm worried about her."

"Well, we all are, considering," Daisy said.

"Has she been having episodes?"

Daisy frowned. "Episodes?" She shook her head. "What are you talking about?"

Was it possible that Daisy didn't know about Gloria's attacks? "What are *you* talking about?"

"Her dad. He had a heart attack. He's staying with her now. Didn't she tell you?"

"No. She didn't say a thing." He rubbed his jaw. "She was just there one minute, gone the next. Without a word."

Daisy sighed. "Typical Gloria. She probably didn't want you to worry. She just goes and tries to handle everything herself, never lets on that she needs help. In fact, when things get really rough, she shuts people out. She's barely taking my calls right now."

"You're kidding."

"Nope. That's why I just go over there and barge in. In fact, I was going to stop by her place after this with a load of baking and some meals. Why don't you take it for me?"

"You sure that's a good idea?"

She gave him a wink. "Positive."

It had been the longest day. Paying bills, working, organizing. She'd managed to keep the panic at bay, but for how long? She'd love to be able to blame Dillon because the attacks seemed to happen more often when he was around, but Gloria knew it was more than that. It was everything. She was overwhelmed and she didn't know where to turn.

Standing outside on the street, she leaned against a truck that was parked outside and stared up at her window. The light was on in the living room.

What the hell was she going to do?

She plodded up the stairs to her top-floor condo and slowly fit the key in the lock. Every movement, every action in slow motion. As if her whole body was screaming at her to turn around and run.

When she opened the door, Gloria heard voices. The TV? Her father rarely watched TV, it was all propaganda, according to him. So maybe he'd fallen asleep. Except that she recognized the voices. One belonged to her father, the other belonged to...

"Dillon?"

"Heya, Red." He held up a shopping bag from Nana Sin's bakery. "Delivery boy."

Her father stood. "Gloria, this is Dillon. Daisy's husband's cousin." He looked pleased with himself as he regarded Dillon over the top of his glasses. "Did I get that right?"

"Dillon and I know each other, Dad."

Dillon cleared his throat. "Your father was just telling me about some of the trouble he's had with the city lately."

Gloria groaned inwardly. She hated when two very separate parts of her world collided. And this collision was on the scale of tectonic activity, resulting in a massive and destructive earthquake.

"They sucked poor Gloria-Rose dry." Her father held up a sheaf of papers. "I'm doing my best to get the money reimbursed. It's not fair. Not fair at all."

Gloria did a double take. Her father was writing the letters to try to get her money back? She didn't know that.

"She works so hard, we both do. Hardworking, tax-paying citizens and they repay us by treating *us* like criminals. It's an injustice."

"Well, thanks for stopping by, Dillon. We'll see you around."

"I invited him for supper. I hope that's okay?" her father said, removing a casserole dish from one of the bags from Daisy.

"No, Dad. That's not okay." She dropped her things on the table, making a loud thud. "Dillon was a client of mine and I think it best to keep business and personal separate."

Dillon arched a brow as if that was news to him.

"Oh." Her father nodded. "That big ranch job, right?" Of all the times for her dad to be paying attention. "How'd it go?" He turned to Dillon. "Did you sell your ranch?"

"Well, now," Dillon drawled as he glanced at Gloria. "Not exactly."

"Dad, Dillon really needs to go. Right?" She narrowed her gaze at him.

"Actually, I was hoping to—"

"I always liked Montana." Her dad smiled with an air of reminiscence. "Your mother and I took you to Yellowstone one summer. Do you remember?"

Gloria shook her head. "No, Dad. We never went to Yellowstone." Was there no end to her father's delusions?

"Sure we did. Though you were only three or four, so I suppose you might not remember." His eyes sparkled with whatever made-up memory was going on in his brain. "We had to put you on one of those little tethers to keep you out of all the steaming pools of water."

"A leash?" Dillon made a sound that sounded suspiciously like a snort. "That sounds about right."

"Hey." She pointed at him to stay out of this.

"Gloria-Rose has always been the independent sort."

"I've seen that side of her."

"Anyway, I've always wanted to go back. Beautiful country out there."

"Right, Dad. Well, Mr. Cross, thanks for stopping by. You probably have a flight to catch." She motioned toward the door with her head, silently willing—no demanding—Dillon leave. But Dillon was ignoring her, because he was studying her father.

"Dillon?"

"You know, I might have a solution for all of us."

Oh, no, he wasn't going to suggest what she thought he was going to suggest, was he? That would be a colossal overstep.

"Why don't you come back to Montana with us? That way Gloria can finish the job, you'll get to see Montana and I can put the ranch on the market. Sounds like a win, win, win to me."

"You didn't finish the job?" her father asked her.

"Dillon Cross, may I speak to you outside for a moment?" Before he had a chance to answer, Gloria took hold of his arm and dragged him to the front door and out into the hall. "What do you think you're doing?" she snarled.

"I'm solving a problem."

"You have no idea what you're proposing. My dad is sick. He can't go traipsing across the country right now."

"Why not?"

"Because Half Moon Creek is in the middle of nowhere. My father needs to be right here, close to a hospital. Besides, there's no way he'd want to leave Chicago."

"Why don't you ask him?"

Dillon's obstinacy filled Gloria with white-hot rage. Not of the panic variety, but of the I-am-at-the-end-of-my-rope-and-am-on-the-verge-of-committing-physical-violence variety.

"Fine," she said. "Let's go." She turned on her heel and strode right down the hall to the stairs.

"Where are we going?"

"I need to show you something."

WHEN DILLON FINALLY found a spot to park the truck, Gloria was striding down the sidewalk toward him, her face pale, paler than he'd ever seen her look. She walked right past him and said, "This way."

He wanted to ask why she'd taken him to some residential neighborhood but decided that silence was the best course of action at the moment. After rounding another block, they passed a multifamily dwelling and then stopped outside a fence. Dillon was so intent on watching the woman, he hadn't been paying that much attention to the houses. She took a deep breath and opened a gate that had a large city-issued sign that read Condemned. On the other side of the gate was a sight that Dillon was unprepared for.

"This." Gloria swept her hand in an arc in front of her. "This is the house *I* grew up in."

To say the yard was a junk heap was being kind. It was a dump. Piles of broken pots, furniture, garbage, signs, wheelbarrows, an old trampoline on its side.

"My dad is sick, and it's not just his heart." Her voice cracked as she spoke.

"Gloria."

"Inside the house, it's even worse." She pointed to the dilapidated structure. "Do you want to see it? Will that help you understand?" Her blue eyes were filled with tears. Her lips pressed together as her chin quivered.

"This is why I can't leave. This is why I have to stay and take care of him. This is why..." She didn't finish the last sentence. As she gazed up at him, the anger was replaced by sorrow. "Go back to Montana, Dillon. I can't help you."

All Dillon wanted to do was wrap his arms around this woman and hold her close. He wanted to touch her soft hair and soothe her. But she was as proud as she was stubborn and he didn't know how to reach her.

How could he leave? But how could he stay? She had enough going on and the last thing Dillon wanted to do was to put added pressure on her.

Not knowing what else to do or say, he whispered, "I'm sorry, Gloria. I really am."

"I know." She reached for his arm and then stopped herself, her hand suspended in midair before it dropped to her side.

He stood for a minute next to her, listening to her ragged breaths, staring into her eyes, hoping to see some indication that what she really wanted was for him to stay.

But there was none. Her eyes may have been filled with tears, but they were also filled with resolve. She'd made up her mind and there was no swaying her.

When he finally came to terms with the fact that she truly needed him to leave, he turned and walked out the gate, having to force his feet to take each step. He stopped to peer over the high fence, needing to see her one last time. A knife pierced his gut to see her standing there, her shoulders hunched, the strong, independent woman he probably cared too much for, broken.

He left, just like you always knew.

She'd waited just long enough to make sure, but as she walked back to her car, she saw that Dillon's rental truck was gone.

She'd shown him her dirty little secret and he'd walked away, just as Gloria knew he would. It was why she'd never brought anyone here. Why she'd never really let anyone get too close.

It was more than embarrassment.

Her life was hell and she didn't wish it on anyone.

Instead of going straight home, Gloria just drove. She needed time to think, to decompress after spending time with Dillon. She needed time to compose herself before going back to her condo, which was feeling less and less like home all the time.

Two hours later, Gloria parked in front of her place, preparing herself to go back upstairs. She didn't think she could feel worse than when she'd parked here two hours earlier. But she did.

After letting herself in, she tripped on a duffel bag that was sitting right at the front door. Beside it was the old typewriter.

What the...

"Dad?" Gloria picked up the duffel and carried it into the living room where her father was busy arranging papers.

He turned. His wispy hair was combed and he was wearing a tattered jacket—one she was sure her mother had bought him over twenty years ago. "Pack your bags, Gloria-Rose."

She dropped the bag by the table. "Why?"

"You have a job to do."

Oh, her father was right about that. She did have a job and that job was standing right in front of her; taking care of her father was the only job that mattered right now. "What job?"

"In Montana."

"We're not going to Montana, Dad."

Her father pushed his glasses up the bridge of his nose. "Yes, we are."

With a half laugh, Gloria muttered, "Don't be ridiculous." She turned and sauntered back to the door.

"What is it about going to Montana that's ridiculous?" her father called.

She stooped to pick up the typewriter—good Lord, it was heavy—and carried it to the kitchen where she hefted it onto the table. "You barely leave your house, let alone the city or the state. There's no way you could handle being on the other side of the country."

The way her father fidgeted and clutched at the papers on the table told Gloria her assessment was correct, which left her feeling both gratified and terribly sad. With a sigh, she made her way into the kitchen and filled the kettle. They both needed a cup of tea.

Or whiskey.

The random thought took Gloria back to the night of the storm.

The cabin.

Dillon.

Warmth radiated through her body as if she had just taken a shot of the strong stuff. From where she stood in her kitchen in Chicago, it seemed impossible that she'd ever been the woman in the cabin, sipping whiskey. Making love.

She shut her eyes, enjoying a moment of remembrance: Dillon's touch, the weight of his body on hers, his mouth, the lovely way he filled her...

She rubbed her eyes. This wasn't helping.

"Dillon should never have come over here."

Her dad glanced up from where he was making piles of paper. "Why?"

"Because." She waved her hand dismissively. "He complicates things."

"How so?" Her father tapped a pile of papers into a

neat bundle and put them in an empty bag she hadn't noticed before.

She crossed her arms. "Dad? What are you doing?"

"Packing."

Gloria groaned. "Seriously? Why are you being so obstinate?"

"Me? *I'm* not the obstinate one." His hand trembled as he pointed at her. "Have you heard yourself lately?"

Gloria was so tired, her laughter bordered on hysteria. "Is that what you think? That I'm the stubborn one in this relationship?"

"Well, yes." Her father blinked at her.

"I may be strong-willed, but *you* are unreasonable."

"Unreasonable? Making decisions for myself is unreasonable?"

Gloria clutched at the kitchen counter as if it was a lifeboat and she was being dragged under. She was so tired of fighting. "Dad, listen—"

"No, you listen. Don't you think I know what you're up to?"

Oh, God. Here came the paranoia, only this time it was going to be directed at her.

"You think I can't take care of myself."

"No—"

"Yes. But, here's the thing. I don't *want* you taking care of me."

She gazed into her father's watery eyes. "I can't leave you. I won't."

"I know. That's why *we're* going to Montana. Together."

"But—"

"No more *buts*, Gloria-Rose." He went back to the table, zipped up the bag with the papers and threw the strap over his shoulder. Then he picked the duffel up from the floor and made his way to the front door. "I'm going to Montana," he called. "I can write my letters there as well as anywhere."

She followed him to the hall, shaking her head the entire way. "Dad, even if we were to go, it's late. I'm sure there's no flights until—"

"The cab is waiting downstairs," he interrupted. "There's a red-eye flight. It's already booked. I may not like computers, but that doesn't mean I don't know how to use one. Now, you can either join me or you can stay here. But I'm going and you can't stop me."

15

"ALL THAT STUFF that happened between you and me? That doesn't have to happen anymore." Dillon said the words quietly as they waited for their bags to arrive on the conveyor belt while Gloria's father was in the restroom. It was the first time he'd had a chance to speak to Gloria in private since being surprised by her and her father in the waiting area at the airport in Chicago.

Man, that was one hell of a surprise.

Though it was pretty obvious that Gloria was *not* in favor of this plan. Her severe expression said it all, as did the ice-cold shoulder she gave him when he sat next to her. The fact she wouldn't speak to him didn't stop him from watching her—the way she doted on her father the entire time, never leaving his side, watching him like a hawk.

Crowds agitated the man. Couldn't blame him, really, airports weren't his favorite place in the world, either.

Now here they were, in the much quieter Butte airport and he waited for some acknowledgment of his statement.

Nothing.

Gloria shifted beside him, craning her neck to see if her bags were coming on the belt. Avoiding his eyes.

He cleared his throat. "Strictly professional, from here

on out." Though what he really wanted to say was, "I can't stop thinking about you. Haven't stopped wanting you. I'd really like to kiss you right now, or at the very least hold you."

But her fierce independence probably wouldn't take kindly to those sorts of sentiments right now.

"I think that'd be best," she said quietly, moving off to grab a bag from the belt.

Her father joined them, smoothing his hair in place, his hands trembling. "I can't believe they wouldn't let me bring the typewriter," he complained for what had to be the hundredth time.

Gloria patiently explained the situation. Again. "You could have put it in checked luggage, Dad."

"I never check luggage."

Dillon caught the eye roll before Gloria said, "We'll find you a new one. Don't worry."

After loading their luggage onto a trolley, Dillon directed them out of the airport to where his truck was parked. "I was thinking we could stay in Butte a few days, go around to some retailers and pick up some of the stuff we need for the place."

With a yawn, Gloria said, "That's a good idea." And proceeded to pull her notebook from her bag, flipping through it. She listed off the items, from appliances to fixtures and "accents"—whatever the hell that was.

"Sounds like a week's worth of work."

"Not if you plan it all out." She turned to him, placing a hand on his sleeve. "Don't worry. I'll take care of it."

Dillon glanced at the hand on his arm. He blinked. Then he raised his gaze and met Gloria's. Ever so slowly, as if she was afraid of waking a sleeping bear, she pulled her hand away.

Her touch had felt so natural and her withdrawal so totally unnatural, but Dillon kept his mouth closed because he had vowed to keep his distance. He had to. For her sake.

TWO DAYS AND what seemed like three hundred stores later, the truck was piled high with as much as they could carry, and arrangements had been made from a few establishments to deliver what they couldn't carry. Some places agreed to rent, other places required them to purchase.

"Your budget can handle it?" Gloria had asked.

Dillon nodded, not bothering to explain that money wasn't an issue. Not for buying furniture, not in the sale of the ranch.

For all intents and purposes, it was like nothing had ever happened between the two of them as they shopped until they dropped. Dillon had never understood that expression until now, and if he didn't see another furniture store for the rest of his life he would be A-OK.

Tuesday morning, they were ready to head to Half Moon Creek and when he went to help Gloria into the cab of the truck, she gave him a cool look and said, "I am quite capable of stepping up into a truck by myself, thank you."

Andy, her father, rolled his eyes. "Welcome to my life," he murmured.

Gloria was quite willing to share the chilly stare with her father, though she eventually gave in when he insisted his daughter take the front seat and that he would sit in the back.

The drive to Half Moon Creek was spent in relative silence, except for the sound of Gloria's father snoring softly from the backseat. Gloria sat still as a statue, looking straight ahead the entire time. Dillon filled the silence with music from the radio, turned low so as not to wake her father, and every once in a while, he thought he heard Gloria singing softly along with the songs. It was a surprise to him that she was familiar with country music, but then, the woman was a source of never ending surprise.

Too soon they were pulling up in front of the Gold Dust.

"Thanks." Gloria turned in her seat and reached into the back to gently shake her father's shoulder. "We're here, Dad."

"What?" Mr. Hurst looked around with a confused expression. "Did I miss the drive?"

"You were tired. If you slept at night, like the doctor told you—"

"Gloria-Rose," her father said, with a warning tone.

Dillon smiled. He liked hearing the sound of her full name.

"I'm going to take this stuff out to the ranch. I'll be by to pick you up in the morning."

"Fine."

He helped them take their luggage inside, but once inside the lobby, Gloria took her father's bag from him, and said, "I've got it."

"Okay." He tipped his hat. "Later, Red."

Her pale cheeks bloomed with color. It was the first indication that he still had any effect on her and it pleased him more than he cared to admit.

THEIR ROOMS WERE located side by side and, after leaving her bag inside her door, she followed her father into his room to help him get settled.

"Quaint place. I like it," he said, looking around.

"You sure you're okay, Dad?"

"Stop doting."

Gloria sighed. "Well, I'm glad you like it, because it's home for the next week or so."

He went straight to the window. "Look at that view."

Gloria joined him. The distant mountains were still

snowcapped, even though it was late spring. "It's nice, isn't it?"

"It's beautiful." He opened the window and took a deep breath. "Do you smell that?"

Gloria sniffed the air. "No. What is it?"

"Nothing. No exhaust, no smog. Just clean air." Her father leaned right out the window, a look of pleasure on his face. Something she hadn't seen in a very long time.

The tension that had been eating away at her suddenly let up, as though it was whisked away on the mountain breeze. Maybe this wasn't such a bad idea, after all.

"Okay, I'm going to unpack and then do some work. We can go down for supper at six."

"Do they have room service?" he asked.

Pausing by the door, Gloria realized that just because he'd opened the window, didn't mean everything was all better. Her father would still be holed up in the room, didn't matter where he was, whether he was at his house or her condo in Chicago, or the Gold Dust Hotel in Half Moon Creek. Nothing had changed.

Gloria sighed. "I don't know, Dad. I can bring something up for you, if you'd like."

She left him in his room and went to settle into hers. It was the same room she'd had last time and it felt as if she'd never left. Yet, everything had changed. She collapsed on top of the bed, lying flat on her back and staring at the molding on the high ceiling.

What the hell was she doing here?

How had she let her father talk her into this?

He didn't give you a choice.

That much was true. Last she checked, blackmail was the opposite of choice. She let out a tired laugh at the thought. Who knew her father was capable of such a thing as blackmailing her into coming to Montana?

The minute Gloria closed her eyes, an image of Dillon came to mind. This time she saw him as he was during their picnic, gazing down at her, the sun creating a glow around him, his shirt unbuttoned. In her mind's eye she saw him smile and heard him say, *All that stuff that happened between you and me? That doesn't have to happen anymore. Strictly professional from here on out.*

Yep. Everything had changed.

GLORIA WOKE FEELING DISORIENTATED. The room was bright and for a moment she had no idea where she was or why. She sat up and the past few days came tumbling back into place. The flight to Montana, the buying trip in Butte. Half Moon Creek.

Her stomach rumbled and she placed a hand on her abdomen to quiet the grumbling before reaching for the phone she'd set on the beside table. Five o'clock. She'd slept for two hours.

Wow. Well, she must have needed it. It had been a trying few days. A trying few weeks. She stood and stretched and then decided to go see what her father was up to. She knocked softly on his door, but there was no answer. She knocked again, a little harder.

Nothing.

Putting her ear to the door, she listened for any telltale signs of activity from within.

Silence.

A terrible sense of foreboding swept all the good feelings away. She tried the door, but it was locked.

"Shit!"

Gloria sprinted down the hall, down the stairs and ran up to the front desk. Thank God it was the same woman who'd checked them in. "I need a key to my father's room. He's not answering and I'm worried."

"Oh," the woman said, nonchalantly. "He left about an hour ago."

"He what?"

"He asked about a secondhand shop. Something about a typewriter."

Gloria tried to calm herself by asking, "What did you tell him?" At least he wasn't dead of a heart attack in his room, but the fact that her father had gone out on his own, in a strange town, in a strange part of the country? Well, it was abnormal.

"Three blocks down Main Street is a place called Second Glance."

"Thanks," Gloria called as she hurried through the lobby and out the door.

She jogged down the street, searching for signs of either her father or the shop, but eventually her steps slowed. This wasn't Chicago. There wasn't a crowd of people moving en masse along the street. There wasn't traffic and horns and lights that might cause confusion for someone like her dad. It was a relatively quiet, sunny day and as she walked, people smiled and said hello to her as if they knew her.

As she passed Mesa Verde, she glanced in through the window and then stopped to stare. Her father was inside, leaning against the counter, talking to Sage.

She opened the door and entered and both her father and Sage turned at the sound of the bells.

"Oh," her father said, "here she is. Sage, this is my daughter, Gloria-Rose."

"We've met," she told Gloria's dad. Sage greeted her with a wide smile. "Nice to see you again. I'm glad you're back."

"How did you know I'd left?"

Sage chuckled softly. "Small town, darlin'."

The use of the endearment reminded her of Dillon. Although, pretty much everything in this town reminded her of Dillon. That was when she noticed the typewriter sitting on the counter. She touched it. "You found a typewriter."

"I sure did," her father said. "It's even in better shape than the last one."

"Do you collect old typewriters?" Sage asked.

"No, I need it for writing."

"Old school." Sage nodded. "I like that. Are you writing a book?"

"Letters." He leaned forward to whisper, "To the government."

Sage whispered back, "I hope you're giving them hell."

"Of course."

The two of them laughed and Gloria watched the interaction with wonder and fascination. Her father was flirting, and Sage was flirting right back.

It was…a miracle.

Sage checked her watch. "Wow. Past closing time."

"Sorry, didn't meant to keep you," her father said, smoothing his hair to the side.

"It's been my pleasure, chatting with you. In fact, if you're not busy, why don't the two of you come for supper?"

Before her father had a chance to reply, Gloria piped up. "That would be wonderful."

DILLON WALKED UP the path to the little blue house on Maple Street and knocked. It had been a while since he'd seen Sage and he was looking forward to her Indian tacos. She made the best fry bread around, crisp and light and salty. Mm-mmm. He rang the bell and Sage came to the door, dressed in a pretty red blouse, long skirt and piles of turquoise jewelry.

"Dillon, come in."

He stepped inside and bent low so she could kiss his cheek. That was when he saw Red, staring openmouthed at him from behind Sage.

"I didn't know you were coming," Gloria said.

He smiled. "I didn't know Sage had invited you, either."

"The more the merrier." Sage glanced at him and winked. Oh, the woman knew exactly what she was doing.

To put everyone at ease, she put them all to work, showing Gloria how to make fry bread, getting Dillon to grate the cheese and set the table and Gloria's father to cut up the tomatoes and lettuce.

The conversation never stopped during dinner, Sage made sure of it, and Dillon had never seen Gloria's father more animated. By the look of wonder on Red's face, she hadn't, either.

"What nation do you come from?" Andy asked during dinner, elbows on table, chin on hands, leaning toward Sage. Rapt.

"The Crow Nation. And…the United States of America." She grinned. "I'm a true American. Part settler, part indigenous."

"Fascinating. How far does Crow Nation territory extend?"

Sage and Gloria's father carried the conversation for the entire meal, and after dinner Gloria insisted on doing dishes. Dillon offered his help and to his surprise, she didn't object.

"Those two have certainly hit it off," Dillon said, indicating the living room where her father and Sage were now having coffee and chatting.

"I know." She smiled, her blues eyes liquid. "It's really nice to see." Just as she placed a washed dish in the rack, he went to pick one up and their fingers tangled. She stilled, her eyes going large and round.

Dillon couldn't help himself from running a wet thumb across the top of her hand. God, he missed touching her.

She withdrew and they finished washing in silence. Once done, Dillon followed Gloria to the living room where she picked up her purse and jacket and said, "Thank you so much for the lovely evening. I'm going to head back to the hotel. I have to catch up on some work."

When her father stood to join her, she said, "Dad, why don't you stay, if it's okay with Sage. I'm fine walking back to the hotel on my own."

"Well—" her father smiled hopefully at Sage "—I wouldn't mind another cup of coffee. As long as it's decaf."

"That would be nice," Sage said. Then she indicated Dillon. "Why don't you walk Gloria to the hotel?"

Dillon thought Gloria was going to go all independent on him again, but she didn't. She nodded toward the door and they left together.

16

THE EVENING WAS brisk with cool air blowing in from the north and Gloria lifted her face, her cheeks warm from doing dishes and probably from thinking about Dillon. She could still feel his touch, a phantom caress across the top of her knuckles. Now, as they walked slowly toward Main Street, she was ultra aware of his hand swinging by his side. What would he do if she reached for him? Would he wrap her hand in his big one or would he push it away?

Or...would he tug her close, tilt her chin up and kiss her?

Who was she trying to fool? She didn't want things to be strictly professional between herself and Dillon. She wanted what they had, the overnighter in a cabin, the freedom of making love on a blanket in a meadow, she wanted to wake up in his arms again.

But then what? How long could that last? A week? Two? A month at most?

Who cares how long it lasts.

For once, Gloria's conscience wasn't snarky. Maybe she shouldn't care how long it lasted. She was so tired of being the responsible one, the efficient one, the sensible one. Maybe, for once in her life, she should be the girl who was carefree, spontaneous and impractical.

"I really like your dad."

She glanced up at him.

"So does Sage."

Man, she loved his voice, deep and low with a bit of a drawl that made it melodic. It reminded her of how much she loved to hear Dillon sing. There was a certain degree of devil-may-care that was required to get up and sing in front of people, which Dillon had. Gloria admired that about him.

"Gloria?"

"Oh." She gave her head a shake.

"Are you upset about your father?"

"No. Not at all. It's just amazing to me. Dad rarely left his house in Chicago."

They walked another half block before Dillon said, "All that stuff with your dad? It can't be easy."

"No. But there are worse things, I guess."

Thankfully, Dillon left it at that and changed the subject. "You know Sage is playing matchmaker between us, right?"

"I figured as much." She glanced up at him, expecting his seductive grin, but instead was greeted with a serious expression. She stopped. "What's wrong?"

"Can I be honest?"

"Of course."

He moved in front of her, facing her. "I want to kiss you right now."

Oh, thank God. She reached for him, gripping the loose material of his jacket.

"But I'm not going to."

Her grip tightened.

"There's something between us."

She nodded.

"I feel it and I figure you do, too."

"Yes," she whispered.

"Even Sage sees it."

"I know."

"So as much as I want to, I don't think we should act on it."

She gazed up at him, not agreeing, not contradicting. She didn't let go of him. The man was articulating all of her thoughts, though he'd come to a different conclusion than her about where they should go from here. "Is it because of my dad?" she asked quietly.

"Is what because of your dad?"

"Your hesitancy to kiss me."

"No." He said the word with such conviction that Gloria believed him. Hard not to when he had such a good, honest face. She couldn't imagine Dillon lying. Reaching up, she touched the whiskers on his jaw. She loved his jaw. So strong, so masculine.

"Red…"

She dropped her hand, smiled and started walking again, because she'd made her decision and if Dillon was reluctant? Well, he wouldn't be for long. He didn't say another word until they were standing on the street outside the hotel. Moving up onto one of the steps so she was on level with him, she turned, rested her hands on his shoulders and said, "Do you know what I think?"

"No."

"I think I'm going to kiss you."

His chest rose. "You're killing me."

"Well, if it's any consolation, you're killing me, too."

"Sounds like a match."

"Yes, it does." She leaned forward and pressed her lips to his and the heavens opened, raining release and freedom on her. She held the sides of his face while he crushed her lips, scalding her with his tongue, letting her know how much he wanted this, too.

Then Gloria pulled away, smiled and said, "Good night, Dillon." She grazed his cheek with the very tips of her fingers. "See you tomorrow."

WHAT THE HELL was Red up to, kissing him like that last night? He'd been trying to hold back for her sake, not his. So, did she want to start up again? Was that it?

If she did, she hadn't said a word about it this morning. Just sat beside him in the truck for the entire drive, smiling like the cat from that damn Disney cartoon where the girl falls down the hole into another world. Well, if it was a game of temptation she was playing, baiting him to see who'd give in to the chemistry they both felt, she'd met her match. Dillon could play that game, too.

Couldn't wait to play.

He shifted in his seat, the crotch of his jeans suddenly feeling too snug. "It's a nice day," he finally said in order to break the silence.

"Sure is." She turned and smiled widely at him, her blue eyes sparkling from the sun shining through the window.

What was that smile about? Was she waiting to see who would crack first and bring up the kiss? That was amateur stuff. Dillon was a professional and he'd see if Red had it in her to keep up.

"I like your outfit."

"This?" Gloria glanced down at her yoga pants and top. "They're nothing special, just my work clothes."

"So you don't actually do yoga?"

She frowned. "Sometimes, why?"

"No reason. Just, you look good in it."

"Thank you," she said hesitantly.

"You're welcome." He waited a few beats before adding, "Those the same pants you wore out here last time?"

"No. But, they're similar." She frowned, probably because she wasn't sure if he was complimenting her or not.

Dillon smiled lazily. "I love those pants."

"Why's that?"

"You kidding? All that bending over? Hell, a man doesn't need a whole hell of a lot of imagination to—"

She hit him on the arm.

"Ouch." He feigned injury. "So you can kiss me but I can't make mention of your snug little pants?"

There it was, peeking up around the collar of her shirt, that tasty pink blush. He would have brought that up as well, just to goad her, but they were nearing the ranch and parked out front was a huge delivery truck with the name of a furniture store they'd visited in Butte.

"That's good timing," she said.

He had to admire her aplomb because she winked at him, as if nothing he said bothered her, and jumped out of the truck before he even shut it off.

EVEN WITH DILLON and Curtis helping the two delivery men, it took an hour and a half to move all the furniture into the proper rooms. They tipped the men before they left and then Dillon helped Gloria unwrap the furniture that had been covered in plastic. She'd been so busy directing everyone, Dillon's suggestive comments from the drive had almost been pushed to the side of her mind.

Almost.

"You did a lot of work while I was gone," Gloria said. The main floor hardwood had been sanded and refinished, making it appear brand-new and the walls had been painted. The furnishings from Sage's shop were in the corner, still covered in tarps and rope and now they had a bunch more stuff, so she could actually start arranging things.

"I've still got to paint the bathrooms and put new shelves up in the larder," Dillon said. "The floors upstairs are done, too."

"What did you do with all the stuff?"

"Dumped most. Donated some. Stored what was left."

Gloria nodded. "Perfect."

Dillon sidled up to her, so close she could smell his aftershave. Wonderfully woodsy and fresh. Mmm.

"You calling me perfect?"

She suppressed a smile. "Not even close." She gave him an elbow to the ribs as he sauntered past, enjoying herself.

"Has anyone told you, you've a tendency toward violence?"

"Do I scare you, big man?"

He ran a hand through his hair, his hat having been set aside while carrying furniture up and down stairs. "For a little slip of a thing, you're awfully jabby."

Gloria could not keep the laughter inside. She rolled her shoulders. Holy. She hadn't felt this good since…when? The last time she was in Montana? No. She felt better than that.

"Give me a hand with this stuff, will you?" She motioned to Sage's covered furniture, bending low to untie the knots. Was it bad that she purposefully aimed her heinie at Dillon and wiggled a bit? After all, they were playing the oldest game known to man, and in the mating game, she wasn't above flaunting her female features.

"You're evil," Dillon muttered, brushing a hand across her hip as he moved past.

"What?" She looked up, batting her eyes innocently, the flesh of her hip tingling from his fleeting touch.

"Naughty, wicked, evil woman."

He untied a length of rope and then wrapped it up in a coil before coming toward her, hand outstretched. "I'll take that."

"What? This?" She fingered the soft, hemp rope she'd just untied that had been used to hold the tarps in place. "What do you want this for?"

"Personal use."

"You've got some." She pointed to the coil in his hand.

"Could use more."

"For what?"

"Do you really want to know?" He came closer, moving nice and slow, took her hands and wrapped the soft rope around one wrist and then the other, binding them in front of her in a loose figure eight.

Gloria's lips parted as air rushed out. "For that?"

"Yep."

Oh, dear. The instantaneous image of herself lying spread-eagle, tied to a bed while Dillon did wicked things to her, stole Gloria's breath.

"You wanna try?" He drew a gentle line from her collarbone up to her cheek.

"I don't know." She wriggled her wrists free from the loose knot, took the rope and wrapped it around Dillon's waist, tugging him close. "Depends on who's doing the tying and who's being tied."

Tilting his head down toward her, he said, "I suppose you think you'd be the one with rope, seeing as you're so bossy and all."

"Maybe. Maybe not. Guess we'll just have to find out."

The sound of boots on hardwood took a moment to register. Dropping the rope, Gloria turned around to find Thaddeus coming down the hall, a big grin on his weathered face.

"Miss Gloria. Ain't you a sight." His Louisiana drawl was thicker than ever.

"How are you doing, Thad?"

"I'm as tickled as a mongoose at a rattler's reunion to see you back here. Anyways, if you have a minute, there's someone I want you to meet."

"Oh." Gloria wiped her hands on her pants and asked, "Who?"

"Sue. She's back."

It took Gloria a moment to remember who the hell Sue was, but then she recalled Thad's story about the dog who played possum and trapped a mountain lion.

Before she took a step, she felt the softly frayed ends of a rope tickle the back of her neck and Dillon's voice, barely above a whisper, "We're not done here, Red."

The shivery sensations running up and down her spine lingered all the way to the shed where Thad motioned for her to enter and crouch beside him.

Puppies!

"Oh, my God! They are so cute." Gloria kneeled beside the border collie cross who was lying on a bed of old blankets and straw, nursing six—no—seven, chubby, squeaking puppies.

"Went out and found herself a man, got herself knocked up real good. But I always knew she'd be back. Sue knows where she belongs."

Gloria laughed at Thaddeus's crass description of Sue's instinctual behavior. "Can I pick one up?"

"They're still pretty fresh. Best leave 'em for another week."

Another week. Would Gloria even be here that long? She stood, wishing that she could take one of the puppies home with her. She'd always wanted a puppy. But would that be fair to the dog? What would it prefer? To live cooped up in a condo over being able to roam freely on a ranch?

She sighed. Okay, no dog.

"Listen," Dillon said, coming up to stand beside her. His eyes still sparkled—an aftereffect of their playful banter? "I've got some chores to do. I'll give you a hand with some of the house stuff when I'm done."

"What do you need to do?" she asked.

"Muck out the stable. Spray down the stalls."

"Why don't I help? Things go faster when we work together."

"You know what 'muck out the barn' means, right?"

"Yep."

"All right, Chicago. You want to help me shovel shit, go get some shit kickers on and you're welcome to it."

THERE WERE STILL a few boxes of Char's clothes left behind and Dillon had stored them in the Quonset with all the other items that he hadn't dumped. It was also the place where Kenny had stored the old furniture from the original house when he'd rebuilt.

"Wow," Gloria said, lifting drop cloths to check the furniture beneath. "There's some nice stuff here."

"Yeah. I meant to tell you about it, but I figured you wanted all new."

She touched a tear in the fabric of an old love seat that looked as if it could have been a hundred years old. "If I had more time, I'd have loved to refinish some of this."

More time. Hell, Dillon wanted nothing more than to grant Red's wish and ask her to stay longer. A month? Two?

Forever?

Shit, man, get your head out of your ass. She'd never want to stay here. And, neither do you, don't forget...

He hefted the box labeled Women's Clothes and opened

it up. Right on top was a pair of boots and he passed them to Gloria. "Will these fit?"

She measured a boot against her foot. "They'll do." She sifted through the open box to see what else was there. "I might change into jeans if there's some in here."

"Need help?"

"You offering?"

"Always." Good Lord, he enjoyed sparring with Red. Whatever had happened to make her change, he liked it. Not that she'd really changed—this was the woman he remembered from the fund-raiser and the night in Chicago. Feisty. Quick-witted. Passionate. Same as the woman who'd holed up with him last time she was here.

Ah, hell. Whatever it was, it didn't matter. All that mattered was that he wanted to keep it up. He wrapped a hand around that narrow waist and tugged her close. "Work first, play later. That's my motto."

"Amateur."

Her hands were on his ass and—holy Hannah—she had a nice firm grip. He grabbed her arms and pulled them back around. "Meet me in the barn." He turned and walked away, calling over his shoulder, "And hurry up about it."

"Hey," she called right back. "Is it just me? Or are you walking funny?"

Dillon let out a laugh as he ambled—yes, he was experiencing difficulty walking—back to the stable, put on some work gloves, got the shovel and wheelbarrow and got to work. The sooner they were done, the sooner they could play.

17

RED JOINED HIM fifteen minutes later.

"There's some gloves in the tack room and the hose is coiled on the wall. Why don't you follow me and hose down each stall after I've cleaned them out?"

"Sounds good, boss."

Dillon paused. "Boss, huh? Is this a hint of things to come?"

She wiped a strand of hair out of her eyes. "Maybe. You'll just have to wait and see."

Okay, he had to curb the banter because otherwise he wouldn't be able to walk *or* work. No, he'd be forced to take Red into the tack room to relieve the pressure behind his fly, in whatever glorious way she saw fit.

The thought of that alone was enough to make him groan in wonderful agony.

Somehow he got his lust-filled cravings under control and he and Red became an efficient team. It didn't surprise him one bit. Red was a hard worker. The surprising part was that she didn't seem to mind getting dirty. He liked that. Hell, he liked pretty much everything about her, particularly the getting dirty part.

She had all these wonderful sides to her. There was the

woman he met over a year ago, dressed to the nines, hair styled, makeup perfect, beautiful. Then there was the one here and now—hair tied up in a bandanna, no makeup, wearing hand-me-down clothes, doing chores and having fun with it.

The first version was hot. The one right here? Smokin'.

A burst of cold water hit him between the shoulder blades.

"Hey! What the hell?"

"Oops." Her eyes were large and round and full of mischief.

He worked his features into a scowl and went on to the last stall, shoveling up the last of the refuse. He was just wheeling it out to the manure pile when she sprayed him again, soaking him.

He set the wheelbarrow down, turned and walked straight into the spray.

Her eyes widened at his approach and she dropped the level of the water so that it hit him square in the crotch. "Need some cooling off?"

"You are so dead," he said, slowly and clearly. Heading right into the spray he came close enough to reach for the hose and easily wrestled it out of her hands.

"Hey!" she complained. "That's mine."

"Mine now." He turned the spray on Gloria and she squealed, covering her face and running in the direction of the tack room. He twisted the nozzle, giving the spray more power and arced it at her as she fled until she found safety inside the room. He waited, just like when he was a kid, waiting to snare a ground squirrel, and sure enough, she peeked around the door, giving him a target for a blast of cold water.

"Truce!" She held a hand out from behind the wall. "We're even now. I call truce!"

Without a word, Dillon turned off the hose and strode to the back of the stable where Gloria was hiding. Rounding the wall, he found her standing there, hands out, huge grin, wet hair plastered to her forehead.

He took her in, sopping clothes sticking suggestively to every curve of her luscious body. "Damn, Red. I like you wet."

"Yeah?" She clutched the front of his shirt and drew him close. "Well, you certainly made me wet."

His hands went around to her backside. Oh, such a nice ass. Perfect amount of flesh for each one of his hands. "How wet?" he asked, pulling her up against him, nice and snug.

"Why don't you find out, cowboy?" She unsnapped the top button of her jeans.

Vixen.

Leaning down, he licked a drop of water from the side of her neck and whispered, "You're playing with fire, Red."

"Don't you think I know that?"

He wedged a knee between her legs and growled when she wriggled against his thigh. "What exactly is it that we're doing here?"

She undid the top button of his shirt and then the next. "I think it's called flirting."

"Yeah?" He backed her up against the wall. "Is that all you want? A bit of flirting?"

Another button undone, then another. "No, Dillon. I want more."

Dammit. Taking those busy hands of hers away from his chest, he pressed them to the wall beside her head and held her there, leaning his weight into her. "When you say 'more,' do you mean this?" He leaned down and kissed her as softly as he could, holding back some because he wanted to make sure of everything before he let loose.

"More." She said the word against his mouth. Soft, sweet and a little demanding, just like her.

Wedging his knee up snug between her legs, he moved it back and forth against the seam of her jeans. "Something like this?"

"That's nice," she whispered, eyes closed, creating her own friction against his knee. "But I could handle a little more."

"Mmm, baby." He nuzzled the side of her neck.

"Man, I love it when you do that."

"Good," he said. "Because I love doing it."

"Dillon?"

"Yeah?" He nibbled his way along her jaw to her ear.

"Take off my shirt."

"Here comes the bossy." Hell, he didn't mind. Saved him from having to ask. Dillon released her hands so he could pull her wet shirt up and over her head. "Damn, woman." He took a moment to look at her: alabaster skin, light pink bra. Reaching behind, he unclasped the strap and tugged it off her. Was it the dampness that made her pretty little nipples stand up like that, begging for a kiss? Or was it him?

If he had any reservations about what was happening, they were gone the minute Gloria put her hands back up against the wall, arching her lovely chest toward him.

"You are one hell of a woman," he groaned, readily giving in to the lure of her naked body, fondling one breast while sucking on the other.

"Dillon…"

He loved the way she said his name, with such wanton desire.

"Promise me something?" The words were soft and breathy.

"Sure thing," he murmured, in the mood to give the woman whatever she wanted.

"Don't treat me like I'm going to fall apart. Treat me like you did that first night, in Chicago."

Releasing her sweet, sweet nipple, he raised his head and caressed her cheek. "What do you mean?"

"I want it wild." She laid her palm against his cheek. "I want it all, with you."

The leash he'd been using to keep himself tethered, snapped. Just like that. And he kissed her with all the fierce abandon he'd wanted to let loose from the moment he'd met her. Melding his mouth to hers, sharing each drop of moisture as if they were drinking from the same well of passion and need, he gave his hands leave to do what they would, caressing, squeezing, handling her body in ways he'd been afraid to.

"Yes!" She bowed against him, revealing that amazing neck and Dillon feasted on her, kissing and licking and biting. Needing her in this savage way just as much as she seemed to need him.

"Gloria? Dillon? Are you in here?"

Dillon stopped. He put a hand to Gloria's mouth to cover her moans, her wide-eyed expression reflected his surprise.

"Are you two back there?" A female voice this time.

Dillon gently released her and Gloria whispered, "It's my dad and Sage." Then she covered her mouth, trying—unsuccessfully—to smother her laughter.

SHE COULDN'T KEEP the giggles inside. Little snorts escaped through her nose and mouth as she fumbled with her bra. Dillon had his shirt buttoned first and stepped out into the aisle of the stable.

"Hey, Mr. Hurst. Sage. What are you two doing out this way?"

"Sage was kind enough to take the day off today to show me around. I was hoping to get a tour of the ranch."

Surely her father must have heard the sounds she was making as she wrestled her wet shirt over her head.

"Well, if you're looking for Gloria," Dillon said, extra loud. "She's probably in the house."

"Nice one," she whispered and then clamped a hand over her mouth because the desire to howl with giddiness did not want to be suppressed.

"We knocked, there was no answer."

"It's a big place. She probably didn't hear you. The door's open, just go on in."

A few seconds later, Dillon leaned his big frame in through the door. "They're gone."

Gloria fell against his chest, smothering her laughter against his damp shirt. "I feel like a teenager."

Chuckling, Dillon said, "You never got caught when you were young?"

Gloria lifted her head. "No. I never brought boys…anyone home." Some of the mirth drained out of her. "Never wanted to."

He squeezed her shoulder. "Well, you have just been initiated into an exclusive club." His voice was jokey but his expression was tender. He tugged on something on the front of her shirt. "Oh, and Red? If you don't want to advertise what was going on in here, you might want to think about turning your shirt the right way around."

Glancing down, Gloria realized the tag was sticking up in front of her. She had her shirt on backward *and* inside out. The ridiculousness of the situation hit so hard, all the giddiness bubbled up and she laughed until she had tears streaming down her cheeks, adding to the dampness of Dillon's shirt. He held on to her, laughing along with her before kissing her soundly and pushing her off in the direction of the Quonset.

"Go dry off," he said. "Meet you at the house."

Gloria couldn't keep the smile off her face. When she found her dad and Sage in the great room back at the house looking around, she ran up to her father, still feeling light and giddy, and gave him a big hug. "Dad! What a surprise."

He hugged her back. "Sage is giving me a tour of Beaverhead County. She's an expert on local history."

"I told him he had to see the ranch." Sage waved to some grocery bags on the table. "And I thought I'd come out and cook up some food." Pointing at Dillon standing nearby, she added, "He works so hard he forgets to eat half the time. And you've probably been too busy to eat or cook, too." She winked.

What did that wink mean? Was it so obvious what they'd been up to? Had she heard what was going on in the stable?

"The best way to see the ranch is on horseback," Dillon said. "Why don't we all go for a ride?"

"Oh, no." Gloria's dad shook his head. "That's Gloria's thing. I don't ride."

"I'll take him around, introduce him to the ranch hands," Sage offered. "Why don't you and Gloria go for a ride. It's a lovely day for it. Stew won't be ready for a couple hours."

Dillon turned to her. "I wouldn't mind. Are we done in here for now?"

No. They weren't done work for the day, but Gloria didn't care because the only thing that would give her more pleasure than a ride was finishing what she and Dillon had started. If she played her cards right, she might get to do both. Then it would be pretty much a perfect day.

THIS WAS EXACTLY where Gloria wanted to be, riding up the slope to the Doghouse. Once the horses reached the top of the slope, he turned the big black stallion he rode, in order to enjoy the vista.

"This is such a nice spot," Gloria said, maneuvering her horse right up beside Dillon's.

"Yep."

She gazed up at him, a portrait of a cowboy staring off into the distance, stoic, strong…incredible. This was where he belonged, as if he was hewn out of the same stone as the mountains, with the clear waters of the nearby creek running through his veins. But her sense of him was more than just the fact that Dillon painted an incredible image. He was an incredible man. The very best. And she, Gloria-Rose Hurst, had it bad for him, there were no two ways about it.

She couldn't remember ever feeling so happy.

"Whatcha thinking, Red?"

Rubbing the horse's neck, she said, "I'm thinking we should take a little break here."

His smile spread slowly. "I'm thinking pretty much the same thing." He dismounted and waited for her to do the same. They tied the horses to a post on the porch so the animals wouldn't wander off, and then Dillon unbuckled a small saddle bag and pulled out two coils of rope from inside.

"Oh." Gloria felt her eyes go wide.

"Just in case." His grin was deliciously wicked and Gloria had to hold on to his arm as they mounted the steps, for balance.

We're not done here, Red.

No. Not done by far.

The second they were inside, Gloria was on him, flipping off his hat and unbuttoning buttons.

"Damn, girl." Dillon helped her with the buttons before helping her off with her shirt. "I thought it was just me that was desperate to get naked again."

"Nope. Now shut up and take off those boots."

Wrapping a hand around her neck, he pulled her close and kissed her first, nice and thorough, before stepping back to comply with her demand. She kicked her boots off, too, and, wearing only jeans and bra, made for the ladder up to the loft. "Is there a bed up here?"

"There is. But what's wrong with down here? Floor not good enough for you anymore, Miss Fancy-Pants?" He helped himself to the back side of her jeans, squeezing flesh and denim together.

"It's a shame not to use a perfectly good bed," she said, leaning into the ladder, enjoying his touch.

"'Perfectly good' is a generous statement in reference to what's up there."

"If it's soft and positioned in a horizontal fashion, it's good enough for me," Gloria said, squealing when Dillon slid his hands around the front of her jeans and unzipped them. She nudged him back with her butt and made for the top, stopping to view the low, cramped space where there was nothing more than a rickety, old brass bed covered in quilts and a simple table on one side and a shelf on the other.

"Told you there wasn't much here." Dillon had to stoop because the ceiling was so low.

"You're up here," Gloria said, yanking him toward the bed. "That's all I need."

"I'll remember that." He pulled her down on top of him and kissed her before rolling her over so he was on top. "These need to come off." He tugged on the waistband of her jeans, pulling them off her hips and peeling them down her legs until she was left wearing only her bra and panties. He stilled. "I don't think I'd ever tire of the sight of you."

That statement sent shock waves through her body but the shock waves turned into all-out quakes of desire when Dillon pulled a length of rope out from behind him. He must have had it tucked into the back of his jeans. He stretched out beside her and dragged the frayed end up her bare legs and belly, then in between her breasts.

"Mmm." Gloria sighed. She wriggled beneath him as he circled one breast and then the other before asking her to remove her bra.

Oh, yes. She eagerly reached around behind and undid the clasp.

She was about to pull it off when he said, "Let me."

Fitting a finger beneath the shoulder strap, he drew it down slowly, revealing her flesh, inch by torturous inch, until her chest was bare. There was enough light in the loft to make out Dillon's expression: serious and tender. With complete concentration he passed the rope over one nipple and then the other. Gloria didn't know if it was the sensation of the soft strands or the visual of Dillon doing what he was doing that elevated her heart rate and had her panting with excitement.

She closed her eyes and gave herself over to sensation, the hemp tracing her rib cage, her shoulders, back and forth across her throat only to be dragged back down all the way to the top of her panties, swishing there before being swept down one leg and up the other.

"Spread your legs," he whispered.

First she lifted her hips in order to push her panties down, and then she spread herself, feeling wanton. Sensual.

Free.

The soft ends barely grazed her inner thighs, a sensation that was part tickle, part pure pleasure. But when those same frayed ends came in contact with her clit, Gloria's body bucked and she reached overhead for the brass bars on the headboard. Needing to hold on to something before her body flew apart from bliss.

"Dillon?" She opened her eyes, though his outline was fuzzy.

"Yeah, baby?" He leaned forward and kissed the top of her mound.

"Tie me up."

His fingers lingered on her thigh, gripping. "How is it that I'm the one with the rope, but you're still the boss?"

She bent a knee, brought her leg up and rubbed his chest with her bare foot. "Because that's the way you like it."

"Damn straight." He grabbed her foot and kissed the instep before moving it aside, giving him room between her parted thighs to lean over her. Gently, oh so gently, he wrapped the rope around one wrist and then the other—a soft hemp caress—before securing it to one of the brass bars. "That too tight?"

She tested it. Her hands could move up the narrow pole but that was it. "Nope."

"You let me know if it gets—"

"Dillon?" Though she couldn't move her hands, she gyrated against him.

"Yeah?" More a groan than a word.

"I want this."

He groaned again and whispered into her ear, "Good, because I am about to torture you."

If torture was the most delicious, exciting thing in the world, then the word accurately described what Dillon was doing. Kissing and licking his way down her body. Nipping on the good bits, her lips, her neck, her breasts, tasting the indent of her navel and biting the taut cords of her inner thighs. The brass bed rattled each time Gloria tugged against it, not because she wanted to break free, simply an involuntary reaction, jerking, bucking and writhing with pleasure, the feeling intensified because she was bound.

Who'd have thought?

But when Dillon parted her legs wide and dipped down to taste her, Gloria lost it all.

"Oh!"

The combination of his whiskers on her skin, his tongue moving her clit back and forth before sucking on her while his thumbs took turns plunging inside—never had she felt such euphoria and it was all intensified by the fact that she was bound and at Dillon's mercy.

Her moans turned to cries culminating in screams as an orgasm rocked its way through her body, making more than one pass up and down her length as Dillon just kept on going. Never stopping, swallowing her orgasm until she was on the verge of another.

"Dillon," she shouted. "Untie. Please! Please untie me."

_18_

AFTER ALL THAT writhing and moaning, he'd thought she was enjoying herself. Had he gone too far? He quickly untied the knots and massaged her wrists to make sure she was okay. "You didn't like it?"

She pressed her palms to his cheeks and kissed him nice and deep. "Are you kidding me?" She took a couple more ragged breaths in between kisses. Against his mouth, she murmured, "I loved it. I loved it _so_ much." Her fingers trailed down his jaw and throat to his chest.

"Then why—?"

"I was going crazy not being able to touch you." She caressed his chest and shoulders and arms. "Like this."

Her lids drooped as the frenetic twisting and writhing of a moment ago drained out of her, replaced by soft, sensual movement. "You're so strong."

No. He wasn't. At least not where she was concerned. He was fucking weak in that department. Her touch was his Kryptonite, and the way she feathered her fingers over his chest and down to his belly left him powerless to move.

At least until she dropped her hand and worked it down the front of his unbuttoned jeans to the fierce erection he was sporting.

"And so hard," she whispered.

Hell, he'd been hard for her since the moment he'd seen her in her fancy city clothes, walking around so officious and efficient but the words stayed deep in his chest, rattling around with each ragged breath he had to remind himself to take. Her fingers trailed up from his shorts, following the line of hair up his stomach and back to his chest. A woman's touch. So soft. So gentle. So erotic.

"Tell me you brought a condom."

He found what he was looking for in the pocket of his jeans. In record time he had his jeans and shorts off and the condom rolled over his length. When he was close, she reached for him and continued that magic touch of hers along his length.

He closed his hand over hers, stilling her movement. "Darlin', I'm so close, you keep touching me like that…"

With a little wiggle and a slight adjustment of her hips, she opened herself to him. "Then what are you waiting for, cowboy."

"This." He rested more of his weight on her and kissed her. So warm, so wet, so inviting. So… Gloria. He explored her mouth like he'd just explored her body, tasting, nipping, sucking her lower lip into his, gentle at first until she started to moan.

It was as though the woman was made for him, reacting to him as if she needed him as much as he needed her. And that need was all consuming yet natural, too, so natural that one little wriggle from her and Dillon found himself pressed right at her center. Instinct took over. He thrust, he had to. There was no choice. All the way. Again, and again. Her moans of pleasure dictating the pace. Slow one second, out of control the next.

"Baby," he growled, as he propped himself up to get better leverage. She wrapped her legs around his waist, meeting him thrust for thrust, taking him deeper into her body with each pass until he swore they were connected in a way that went beyond the physical, in a way that meant the connection was permanent, could never be broken. That this was where he belonged.

And this was where she belonged.

GLORIA LAY FOR a few blissful minutes, ensconced in Dillon's arms, too boneless to get up, too content to even want to.

"We best get back before your father calls out a search party."

Rubbing her cheek against his chest, she sighed. "I guess you're right. Though I feel like I could lie here forever."

For all that Dillon said they should get up, he didn't move except to stroke her hair and back. "You ever think about living anywhere other than Chicago?"

Gloria held her breath. What was Dillon asking? "I don't know," she finally replied. "I've never given it much thought."

Before now.

She waited for his follow-up question, but it didn't come. He just groaned and carefully rolled out from under her. The roof was so low, he was having trouble getting dressed, so he grabbed his clothes and said, "I'll wait for you outside."

She found Dillon on the porch, sitting on a log swing built for two, staring out at the view. She sat down beside him, wrapped her arms around him and said, "Thank you."

"For what?"

"For being you." They sat on the swing, holding hands in silence. Completely comfortable.

"Dillon?"

"Yeah?"

"Why are you selling the ranch?" Gloria turned to gaze up at him. His hat sat on the bench beside them so she was able to see his eyes.

"I told you. I'm on the rodeo circuit most of the year. Never here."

"Hasn't your back had enough bull riding?"

He turned his head, a single eyebrow arched.

"You groan every time you bend. Seems like it gives you a lot of trouble." Her hand moved to his thigh, stroking the denim that covered his powerful muscles. "Plus, you love it here. I can see that you do."

He blinked but there was no expression. His features were granite. Stony.

"What's the real reason?"

By the way his chest rose, he was drawing a deep breath, yet he stayed silent.

Finally, just when she didn't think he'd answer, he said, "I don't deserve it."

She raised her gaze back to his face. "What do you mean?"

He rubbed his jaw and turned away, as if he couldn't bear her looking at him. "Let's just say that I've done things that make it impossible for me to keep this place. Things I can't take back, can't even ask forgiveness for." Picking up his hat, he fit it on his head. "And that is the end of the story."

DESPITE WHAT HE said about not keeping the ranch and that that was the end of the story, the idea of keeping the ranch was sure making the rounds inside of his head. That was all Dillon thought about on the ride back to the main house no matter what he did to get rid of it. He was thankful for Sage and Andy's presence just to give him a little peace of mind.

"Just in time," Sage said when she saw him enter the kitchen. "The bannock is fresh out of the oven."

"Smells delicious." He kissed her cheek and she patted his.

"Where's Gloria?" her father asked as he rifled through drawers, apparently looking for cutlery to set the table.

"She's changing, I think."

Andy found what he was looking for and he motioned to the dining room. "Can you give me a hand?"

Uh-oh. Didn't matter how old you were, being pulled aside by the father of the woman you were sleeping with made a man feel jumpy.

"Whatever it is you're doing with my daughter, keep doing it," he whispered.

"What do you mean?"

Andy glanced toward the hall, as if he wanted to make sure he wouldn't be overheard. "I've never seen her so happy. Not since her mom died." He thumped Dillon on the back. "You're a good man, strong enough to stand up to her." He winked. "I'm giving you my blessing."

Dillon didn't know what came over him, but in some weird spontaneous act, he gave Gloria's dad a hug, thumping his back the way he'd just done to Dillon, even though he wasn't sure if he was up to the task of what Andy had given his blessing for.

"Wow, it smells good in here," Gloria said, entering the room seconds later. Had she overhead the conversation? Her skin was pink, but that could easily be from washing up, or remnants of his kisses and whiskers. Mmm. Now that was a nice thought. A whisker burn on her neck. From his whiskers.

Mine.

Whoa. He gave his head a shake.

Easy, Dillon. She may feel like yours in the here and now, but then what?

Minutes later, the food was laid out and everyone sat around anxious to eat, the second time in as many days that the four of them had sat down to a meal together. Days ago they were all relative strangers and yet, sitting here sharing a simple meal felt comfortable.

"Thank you so much, Sage," Gloria said, dishing a huge helping of stew onto her plate. "I am starving."

"Well, you've had a…busy day." Dillon emphasized his words with a little footsy action beneath the table.

The sparkle in her eyes and blush in her cheeks were all the gratification he needed. She covered up what was going on by turning to Sage. "How's business these days?"

"Slow," Sage said. "Thank goodness for the internet."

"You're on the internet?" Gloria's dad set his fork down, looking startled. "Don't you worry about being exposed? Exploited? Scrutinized?"

Obviously, Sage found Andy's questions amusing, because she laughed heartily. "Oh, Andrew. This is the twenty-first century. It's the way of the world. I learned a long time ago that there's no sense holding on to the past, no matter how much you don't want things to change." She smiled at him and the newfound fondness did not go unnoticed.

Gloria's father smiled back and Dillon could see from his expression that he was taking in what she'd said as if it was a completely new and foreign concept to him, one he'd have to think about seriously.

"If not for the internet, I'd have had to close a long time ago. Internet sales make up 60 percent of my revenue. Only 40 percent are walk-ins. This weekend counts for about half of that." She turned to Dillon and pointed her fork at him. "Speaking of this weekend, don't forget you're on the list to help set up tomorrow."

"How could I forget."

"What's going on this weekend?" Gloria asked.

"The county fair and rodeo," Dillon supplied.

"Are you riding?"

He nodded. "Yep. This'll be my fifteenth year straight. Wouldn't miss it."

WITH ALL FOUR of them cleaning up, dishes took only a few minutes and strangely, Gloria wished it would have taken a little longer. There was something so nice about working together after a delicious meal.

"Do you need more help setting up tomorrow?" her father asked Sage.

"Of course. We always can use a few more hands."

He set the dishcloth down, revealing his hands. "These are yours to command."

Grasping hold of them, Sage said, "Thank you. I appreciate it."

Gloria leaned against the counter, wiping out a pot, watching the interaction between Sage and her father closely. For the first time in a few days, she noticed that her father's personal tics—playing with his glasses, smoothing his hair, blinking—were less pronounced. Was it Sage? Was it getting out of Chicago?

Was it Montana?

Then, out of nowhere, a memory jostled its way into her mind: she was sitting on her father's lap in the sunshine waiting for a geyser to shoot hot water into the air, accompanied by a vague recollection of a sour sulfury smell.

"Dad?" Gloria said. "When we were at Yellowstone, did we see Old Faithful?"

"We sure did. Stayed the whole afternoon. You sat on

my lap, patient as anything, waiting for it. Every time it went off, you clapped."

"Yeah," she said. "I remember." She blinked and looked at her father, seeing the man he used to be, not the one he'd become in the past twenty years.

Lowering her eyes, she finished the pot and turned her back, needing to hide the tears pooling in the corner of her eyes.

"I hope you don't mind if we get going," Sage was saying to Gloria's dad, "but I don't like driving in the dark."

"Me, neither," her father said.

After kissing her father and Sage goodbye, she and Dillon stood on the porch, watching them go.

"So, what do you think? Should we head back, too?" Dillon asked after they'd watched the truck turn off the lane onto the main road.

"No." Gloria gazed up at him. "I think we should get some of that new bedding we bought, make up one of the beds in a guest room and test out one of the new bed frames."

He grinned wide. "I like the way you think, Red."

"And, Dillon?" She grabbed his belt loops and tugged him close. "Bring the rope."

19

DILLON LEFT GLORIA SLEEPING—not an easy thing to do when she looked so peaceful and beautiful curled up in that big bed—and drove back to Half Moon where setup for the fair had already gotten underway. He spent the morning putting up tents and stages, running cords for sound systems and setting up lights. He was in the midst of unloading chairs from a flatbed truck when Max Ozark came over to lend a hand.

"Good news, Dill. We've got a bite."

"A what?"

"An offer." When Dillon shook his head in confusion, Max added, "On the ranch. You know? That big piece of property you're trying to sell?"

"But Gloria's not done fixing it up."

"Don't matter. I put the listing as is, using the shots I took that first day, remember?"

"Yep. I remember." Dillon suddenly felt itchy. "Who wants it?"

"A family who runs dude ranches up in Canada and Colorado."

"You're kidding." Dillon set down the pile of chairs

inside the tent for the beer garden and scratched his jaw. "How's the offer look? They trying to lowball us?"

"It's decent." Max dropped a pile of chairs beside his. "I've checked them out, they run quality establishments. Could be good for Half Moon, bring in some tourism dollars."

"You think I should take it?" Dillon asked hesitantly.

"I do. If you still want to sell, that is."

"Of course," he answered quickly. "I just didn't think it'd happen so fast. I mean, I thought it would take more work."

I thought Gloria would get to stay longer...

"Come by my office on Monday, we'll look it over."

"Sounds good." Dillon smiled tightly and motioned to the other side of the grounds. "I'm off to help Sage with the arts and crafts tables. I'll talk to you about this later."

As he walked, the coffee and doughnut he'd eaten for breakfast churned into a solid mass, sitting heavy in the pit of his stomach. Instead of heading to the arts and crafts tables, he went the other way and headed toward the rodeo grounds. Walt was on a tractor, grading the ring, and there was a crew sweeping the stands and repairing the gates.

"Hey, tough guy. Ready to get your ass whipped in the ring tomorrow?"

Dillon turned around and troubling thoughts about the ranch were momentarily forgotten. "Colton? What the hell?"

After a brief back-thumping greeting, Colton said, "What? Can't a brother come back to his hometown to show up his washed-up older brother?"

Dillon jabbed his brother playfully in the arm. "Cocky as ever."

"Big and stupid as ever," Colton replied with a laugh. He glanced around the grounds. "So, where's the bet?"

"The what?"

"I was in Chicago a couple days ago, and I went to the gym. Saw Jamie and he mentioned something about a girl and a bet. He said you owe him two hundred bucks, by the way."

Shaking his head, Dillon laughed. "Her name's Gloria and she's working at the ranch right now." Wrapping his arm around Colton's neck, and getting his younger brother in a headlock, he said, "And Jamie doesn't know shit, because I won that bet."

His brother was strong and wily and easily got himself extricated from the headlock. "Whatever you say, big brother." He shoved him. "How about taking a break and finding us a beer tent. I'm parched."

"Plenty of time to drink after the work's done."

Colton groaned at the sky. "That's right. Work first. Play later. Blah, blah, blah. You're so friggin' boring."

"And you're a lazy ass."

"Hey. I'm helping. I'm taking care of the livestock." Colton elbowed Dillon in the ribs. "Catch up later?"

"Absolutely."

"Oh," Colton called, before Dillon could take off. "Guess who else is back in town?"

"Who?"

"I'll give you a hint—it's a woman, she's from around here, and you know her pretty damn well."

Dillon's stomach sank.

"By the look on your face, I'd say you guessed it. Saw Char singing in the Prospector last night during open mic. Heads-up, she's looking hotter than ever." Colton made a clicking sound with his tongue and winked. "Later, Dill."

Dillon stood rooted to the ground. What the hell was Char doing back in town?

GLORIA HAD A vague recollection of Dillon kissing her before he left and whispering something about…hmm? What was it? She sat up and found his note on the table beside the bed.

> Thanks for last night. And yesterday. I'll be back to pick you up at six.
> XX Dillon

Clutching the note to her chest, Gloria jumped out of bed, energized to get to work. Seriously, she felt as though she'd spent the night plugged in and was fully and completely charged…for everything! The first thing she did, after showering, was make a list of all the things that needed to get done and, to her delight, as she came down the stairs the bell rang and two more delivery trucks were parked out front.

Perfect!

That would be the last of it. The final deliveries contained all the smaller furniture and accents, the lighting and carpets, all stuff she could handle on her own. She directed the men to put everything in the corresponding rooms and after they left made a quick breakfast of toast and eggs—all that was available in the fridge—and got to work.

Her day was spent making beds, hanging new window coverings, hanging art, arranging accents on new side tables and shelves. She went out to the field and found wildflowers and grasses, and cut them and put them in the new vases. It was five thirty before she finished, and she gazed around at all she'd achieved, feeling a wonderful sense of accomplishment.

This had to be some of her best work. When staging, it was important that the house looked attractive, spacious but also not too specific, so the buyers could picture their own belongings inside. This place was slightly different. She wanted whoever bought this place to come in and want it, as is. Filled with the furnishings she'd chosen because this wasn't some generic, cookie-cutter house. This was a unique opportunity and everything she chose was with the ranch in mind. Now that everything had come together, the big ranch house looked like more than just a potential guesthouse.

It looked like a home. A place people could be comfortable and happy.

"I could be happy here," she said to herself and then let out a big breath.

Dillon was supposed to be by to pick her up in half an hour and she wanted to look her best for him. However, all she had here was her yoga stuff, so she went back out to the Quonset and was about to go through the box of clothes, when she got distracted by all the other things stored in the big shed. Tables, chairs, china cabinets, lamps. Sure, some of the stuff was garbage, but some of it was good solid furniture that could easily be refinished.

She had a vision of herself making this space into a workshop and selling antiques online, while helping Dillon run a dude ranch, taking people out on trail rides, cooking up big meals and eating in the dining room, meeting people, sharing the beauty of this place.

"Oh, my God. Stop." She recovered the antique hutch and went back to the box of clothes. "I've got to stop thinking that way." Picking up the entire box, she carried it inside and up the stairs to the room she'd shared with Dillon last night. When she walked in, she cried out and dropped the box.

Dillon was lying on the bed, boots crossed at the ankles, hands behind his head, staring up at the ceiling. He turned his head at her cry and said, "Sorry. Didn't mean to startle you."

"It's okay." She pretended to frown as she pointed at his feet. "Boots off the brand-new comforter, cowboy."

He sat up, placing his boots on the floor. "Sorry." Strangely, his expression seemed serious.

She frowned. "Everything okay?"

He grabbed his hat from the bureau and fixed it back on his head, "Yep. Everything's great." Looking her up and down, though not in the suggestive way as he'd done yesterday, he said, "You ready to go?"

"Not quite. I need to shower."

"Okay. I'll wait downstairs." He smiled and walked out. No playful banter, nothing about joining her in the shower. No mention of christening the other seven bedrooms that she'd spent all day making up.

She followed him down the stairs. "What's going on?"

"Nothing," he said over his shoulder as he continued through to the great room. Then he added, "The place looks amazing, by the way. I don't know how you did it, but it looks completely different. Brand-new."

"Thanks," she said with a frown, because it was a compliment but…not really, because his voice was flat and his expression bordered on displeasure. As if he didn't like what he was seeing.

"Are you unhappy with the choices I made, now that you see everything in place?" she asked, trying to see the room through his eyes.

"No." He came up to her, took her hands in his big ones and squeezed. "Honest. It's amazing."

"So, why are you acting weird?"

"Am I?"

She grabbed the rim of his hat and took it off. "Look at me."

His face was stoic and inscrutable. Same as he'd looked on the porch swing yesterday.

"Yes, you're acting weird. Is it something I've done?"

He shook his head. "It's not you at all. I'm just distracted. The fair brings back lots of…memories. Plus, my brother's back in town." He shrugged as if that explained everything, which it didn't at all.

"Oh," Gloria said, still scrutinizing Dillon for some sign of what was really going on. "I look forward to meeting him."

For the first time, a playful smile lit his features. "Well, he considers himself to be something of a ladies' man, so beware."

Gloria returned the smile, but it didn't seem to have any effect on him as he checked his watch.

"You know, I can shower back at the hotel."

"You don't mind?"

Yes.

"No. Just need to grab something from upstairs." She wanted to bring the box of clothes, figuring there was something more fitting for a country fair and rodeo inside that box than what she'd brought from Chicago, but she was distracted by Dillon's strange behavior.

A few minutes later, they were headed back to Half Moon Creek. The road to town was becoming familiar and Gloria recognized more than one landmark as they drove—the old barn just past the washed-out bridge, the wind-twisted tree that marked the next turnoff. The cattle-crossing sign that was the last sign before turning toward Half Moon Creek.

With ten miles left to go, Gloria placed her hand on Dillon's thigh, slowly sliding her hand higher, making small circle as she went. Just when she was about to reach the top, he stopped her. "What are you doing, Red?"

"This is my way of asking you to come up to my room at the Gold Dust."

"You know those walls are paper-thin." He brought her hand to his mouth and kissed her knuckles. He smiled, and to her relief, it appeared genuine. "I hate to tell you, but you're loud." He placed her hand back in her lap. "You want to broadcast what we're up to, for the whole county to hear?"

"Well," she hedged. "You could always invite me to your place."

"Tempting, but I live in a trailer. Sound proofing isn't much better there." He patted her leg. "Besides, I'm riding tomorrow. I need an early night and if memory serves, sleeping beside you is not conducive to a full night's sleep."

Too soon, Dillon stopped in front of the hotel, got out and opened her door. "I'm riding at noon. I hope you'll watch."

"Of course I will."

"Can I carry this up?" He indicated the box on the backseat.

"I've got it, thanks."

"Okay." He leaned in and kissed her softly on the cheek before retrieving the box and passing it to her. "See you tomorrow, Red." He went back around to the driver's side, got in and drove off, leaving Gloria to wonder, *what the hell is going on?*

GLORIA SAT IN the bleachers with Sage beside her and her father on the other side of Sage. The fact that her father and Sage were holding hands did not go unnoticed. She smiled to herself, despite feeling less certain about her own love life at the moment. But once the bull riding began, Gloria started to wonder if she'd been overreacting to Dillon's distant behavior last night. She'd never seen anything like it. Men riding these enormous, muscle-bound animals that were intent, not only on bucking them off, but on potentially goring them to death once they were on the ground. The riders' bodies were jerked and whipped around as if they might snap in two at any second. No wonder Dillon's back ached all the time. No wonder he wanted to rest last night.

When they called Dillon's name—five-time national champion—as the next rider, Gloria's stomach roiled with a combination of excitement and worry.

Placing her hand on Gloria's knee, Sage said, "He'll be fine."

How had she known Gloria was worried?

The horn sounded, the gate opened and Dillon came out riding the biggest bull she'd ever seen. The thing didn't just buck, it twisted in the air, kicking and turning, jumping and spinning. A millisecond before the eight-second horn sounded, Dillon got bucked off.

The crowd groaned in unison. Quick as a flash, the rodeo clown distracted the bull while one of the riders removed the belt around the bull's middle, corralling the animal out of the ring while Dillon slowly climbed to his feet, waving his hat at the crowd as he limped slowly out of the ring.

The next rider was Dillon's brother Colton. Though his bull was smaller, its moves were even more dramatic, leaping high into the air and kicking almost vertically. Colton easily completed the eight seconds before jumping off to a thunderous applause.

"That boy's a show-off," Sage said with a chuckle, as Colton did a running flip in the ring after his ride.

Gloria tapped Sage's arm. "I'm going to go see how Dillon's doing."

"You do that."

She found him out behind the rodeo ring, sitting on a bench, drinking a bottle of water.

"Hey," she said, as she approached. "You okay?"

"I've been better." He tried to smile but it was more of a grimace than anything. "I've got to stretch out my back before my next ride tomorrow."

"You can't be serious," Gloria said. "You're not riding again."

"That's right, old man." A young carbon copy of Dillon approached from Gloria's right. "Listen to the woman. She knows what she's talking about."

Dillon stood, groaning. "Colt, this is Gloria." He jabbed Colton in the shoulder with a playful punch. "Gloria, this is my pain-in-the-ass brother. Colton."

"Howdy, miss." He removed his hat and grinned, revealing an adorable dimple in his right cheek. "It's a pleasure to make your acquaintance."

Gloria shook his hand. "I bet you break a lot of hearts."

"You're going to make me blush." He winked before settling his hat back on his head in a move that reminded her of his older brother. "And you are a stunner. When you tire of the old stock—" he indicated Dillon with a movement of his chin "—think about giving the better Cross brother a try." He laughed before walking off with a loping, bowlegged stride.

"He is something else."

"Yep." There was fondness and amusement in Dillon's tone. "Please don't blame me for his upbringing, I had no part in it."

"Yeah, right."

His chuckle turned into a groan as he leaned on the fence post. "Listen, Red. I gotta go take some pain meds before I seize up any worse than I already have. I'll catch up with you later, okay?"

"Yeah, sure."

He kissed her cheek and moved off toward the first-aid tent, walking slower than she'd ever seen him move before.

She touched her cheek. That was twice he'd done that, just a little peck on the cheek, nothing more. She frowned and then caught herself. The man was in pain, of course he wasn't feeling amorous. It was nothing to worry about.

Still…

Gloria spent the remainder of the day checking out the fairgrounds that a couple of days ago had been an empty field and now was filled with colorful tents, amusement park rides, food booths and stages. It was a wonder to her. Animals, food, art and amusement all in one place for one weekend only. She'd spent part of the afternoon with her father and Sage, until it was Sage's turn to man a concession stand and her father chose to stay and help.

By six o'clock, she was exhausted and completely full, having sampled two of the ten chilies in the chili competition, eaten beef on a bun and topped it off with a candy apple.

She loved it. Gloria only wished she could share the experience with someone.

Not *someone*, Dillon.

All day, her gaze surveyed the crowd, looking for him, but she hadn't seen any sign of him since his ride, no message from him, either.

It was three blocks back to the hotel, and Gloria headed there, intent on freshening up, but found the hotel and saloon packed with people crowded inside and out where a tent had been set up. At one end, was a stage where an attractive woman with long, dark hair and a tight, short skirt sang a mean rendition of Carrie Underwood's "Little Toy Guns."

"Gloria, over here." Max Ozark, the real estate agent,

was sitting at a table where there was still an empty seat. "You look like you could use one of these." He handed her a red plastic cup filled to the brim with beer.

"Thanks, Max." She sipped the cool draft, not even realizing how thirsty she was.

"So, did Dillon tell you?"

"Tell me what?"

"We've got an offer. It looks good."

The beer turned to acid on her tongue and she set the cup down. "No," she said. "He didn't."

"He's going to sign on Monday."

Monday? That meant her work was done. She could go home.

Gloria pushed the beer away just as Max said something else, but she was unable to make it out because suddenly the crowd went crazy with applause as the singer finished the song.

"Hey y'all, I'm in the mood for a duet."

"I'll sing with you, Char!"

"Thanks, Eddie. But, I actually had someone special in mind."

"I'm special, Char!"

"You certainly are, Walt."

The crowd lit up with laughter. This was what it was like, living in a small town where everyone knew everyone. Normally she would have enjoyed the banter between members of the community, but now it only made her feel left out.

"How about my high school sweetheart?"

More cheers went up from the crowd.

"Dillon Cross, you out there?" She put a hand to her forehead and searched the crowd. "There you are! Come sing with me. It's been too long, darlin'."

From the other side of the tent, Dillon made his way to

the stage and Gloria felt as if someone stabbed her from behind. The second he was onstage, Char wrapped her arms around him and hugged him. Close and for much too long.

"This is an oldie, but a goody," Char said, once she finally released Dillon. She nodded to the man working the karaoke machine and an old Kenny Rogers-Dolly Parton tune started up.

Gloria felt as if she'd been turned to stone. This was *Char.* Kenny's ex-wife. And she sang to Dillon as if she meant every word she said. Smiling at him, flirting with him.

And Dillon sang right back.

Let's just say that I've done things that make it impossible for me to keep this place. Things I can't take back, things I can't even ask forgiveness for.

Had something happened between Char and Dillon? Was Dillon still in love with her?

Oh, God. Gloria stood, needing to escape.

Making her way through the crowd was no easy feat as she twisted one way and then another, feeling a strange affinity for the bulls who only wanted to buck the person off their backs.

"Miss Gloria." A familiar Louisiana drawl stopped her. "You are looking as pretty as ever."

Thad was there, scrubbed and shaved, wearing a new shirt and a lopsided grin.

"Hi, Thad." Gloria squeezed his arm as she tried to ease past but Thad held on to her elbow.

"You remind me of Sue, you know that?"

"I remind you of a dog?"

"Sure. Smart, loyal. The kind of companion a good man needs." He let her arm go to adjust the collar of his shirt. "Did I ever tell you the story about how Sue trapped a mountain lion?"

"Yes." Gloria smiled, or tried to.

"Thought I did. It's a good story, ain't it?"

She felt her brows pull together when she realized that Thad wasn't looking at her, but was gazing up at the stage where Dillon and Char were singing.

"All right, miss. Have a good night and I'll see you when I see you."

20

GLORIA NEEDED SOME SPACE. She needed room to breathe and figure things out so she walked up and down the streets of Half Moon Creek. The place was deserted because everyone was at the fairgrounds or the saloon.

Could she have been wrong about Dillon? Was Char the reason he'd been acting so distant the past couple of days?

It's not you at all. I'm just distracted. The fair brings back lots of...memories.

As in memories of Char?

Gloria didn't know what to think, the only thing she knew was that she loved Dillon, she didn't want to leave Half Moon Creek, and now chances were Dillon was in love with another woman.

Approaching the hotel from the alley in hopes of avoiding the crowd, Gloria ran into the one person she least wanted to see. Char stood out on the back stoop, smoking.

"Excuse me," Gloria said, trying to step past to get inside.

Char stepped in front of her. "You must be Gloria." Smoke wafted into Gloria's face as Char spoke.

"And you're Char."

Char dropped the cigarette and ground it beneath the

heel of her boot, all the while scrutinizing Gloria. "Nice dress."

Looking down at herself, Gloria realized she was wearing Char's clothes. Oh, God. She wanted to rip the dress off right this second and burn it. She elbowed past Char and mounted the steps to the hotel.

"You know you're nothing more than a bet, right?" The other woman spoke from right behind her.

Gloria stopped and turned. "What?"

"Didn't Dillon tell you?" She flipped her hair. "He and his cousin made a bet about you. His cousin didn't think you'd fuck him. Dillon said you would." She laughed as if it was a big joke.

"Where'd you hear that?" Gloria asked, her teeth clenched. White-hot rage whipping through her.

"Dillon's little brother."

It couldn't be true, could it?

As if she was reading her thoughts, Char put a hand to her heart. "Don't believe me? Ask Dillon. I've known him forever and the man can't tell a lie to save his life." She winked. "He and his cousins were always making bets when they were kids. Far as I can see, the man hasn't changed at all."

Gloria fisted her hands so tight, her fingernails bit into her palms as she struggled to control herself.

Adjusting the microscopic skirt she wore, Char said, "By the way, I'm moving back. I always liked Kenny's ranch and I heard you fixed it up real nice."

"If you liked it so much," Gloria said quietly, "why'd you leave?"

"Now that's the question, ain't it?" Char jostled herself in front of Gloria. "I married the wrong cowboy." She licked her full, pouty lips. "I was Dillon's first and I plan on being his last. Know what I mean?"

Of course Gloria knew what she meant—the woman had absolutely no subtly. Gloria had the urge to slap the fake smile right off the woman's face. But then, another idea came to her.

You remind me of Sue.

Straightening her shoulders and holding her head high, she said in the sweetest voice she could muster, "My work's done here and I'm heading back to Chicago." She paused. "The ranch has an offer and Dillon plans on selling, so you better act fast before it's too late."

Char's eyes widened. "Thanks for the heads-up, darlin'." She patted Gloria's cheek. "You're okay."

It took everything in her not to turn her head and bite.

WHERE THE HELL was she? She wasn't up in her room, she wasn't in the saloon or the tent. He hadn't seen her all day and he'd left his phone at home so he couldn't text her. Catching sight of Colton standing in the beer line, he worked his way over to him and tapped him on the shoulder.

"You seen Gloria?"

His brother's typical cocky grin looked sheepish. "Yeah."

"Where is she?"

Colton rubbed his cheek. "Dunno. She kind of stormed off."

"Why?"

"Probably because she asked me if she was a bet."

Dillon shook his head in disbelief. "What? How the hell would she have known to ask that?"

"I may have accidentally said something to Char the other night and then…well. You know Char."

"Dammit." Dillon pushed past his brother, his stomach

in knots. Surely Gloria wouldn't believe the thing about the bet, but then, what else had Char told her? Everything?

"By the way, Char's looking for you," Colton called after him.

His vision became infused with red as he elbowed his way through the crowded tent, pausing when he saw Sage and Andy slow dancing to a fast song on the dance floor. He bulldozed his way over to them, putting a hand on both their shoulders at once.

"You seen Gloria?"

Sage nodded. "Yep. She asked to borrow my truck."

"Why did she want your truck?" Was she on her way to Butte, intent on flying back to Chicago?

"Something about staying out at the ranch one last time."

Dillon didn't wait to hear another word. He pushed his way through the mob, not caring when people complained about his rough exit.

A sense of panic filled him as he drove along the dark road. Visions of a truck flipped over made him drive slowly, scanning the ditches along the side of the road. For all she was independent, Gloria didn't know the first thing about driving these country roads alone and at night. When he got to the ranch, he breathed a sigh of relief to see another truck, except as he parked beside it, he realized it wasn't Sage's and he didn't recognize it.

Shit!

Had something happened?

He ran up the step, wrenched the door open and collided with a woman on the other side. Her arms wrapped around his neck and her mouth met his, wet and tasting of secondhand smoke.

Dillon jerked back. "Dammit, Char, what are you doing here?"

"What do you think?" She grabbed his shirt and pulled him close, rubbing her chest against his. "I'm coming home."

"This isn't your home."

"But it could be. It's a nice place, Dilly. We could be happy here." She gyrated some more, as though she was an exotic dancer and he was a pole.

Not sexy.

"Don't you remember how good we were together?" Her voice took on a petulant tone. He recognized it as the voice she used to get whatever she wanted. God. How could he have been so blind for so many years?

"That was a long time ago."

"No. It was only a few years ago when we went by your old place, remember? It was so beautiful. That's why I had to leave Kenny. I didn't know how to make sense of it all. But Kenny's gone now and you and I can be together." She smiled up at him. "I haven't stopped thinking about that night…" She touched his face and her fingers smelled like tobacco. "Or you."

"I haven't stopped thinking about it, either, Char. Wish I could, but I can't."

GLORIA HAD HEARD him plain as anything.

I haven't stopped thinking about it, either, Char. Wish I could, but I can't.

The statement was a knife to the gut, piercing and crumpling. Could she have been wrong about Dillon? Worse, could *he* be fooled by the likes of Char? Two seconds in the woman's presence and her character was clear. She was an exploitive, self-serving gold digger. The kind of woman who used her body and whatever other resources she had to get what she wanted.

"Oh, Dillon!" The sound of Char's overzealous enthusiasm turned Gloria's stomach.

"No, Char. You don't get it. I haven't forgotten, but I wish I could because I've regretted messing around with my best friend's wife every single day since it happened."

Gloria gripped the wall.

"You don't mean that." Char's voice took on a whiny tone.

"What happened between us was a mistake."

"How can it be a mistake when we love each other?"

"I don't love you."

"Yes, you do. C'mon, Dilly. We're supposed to be together. We've always known that."

"No."

Gloria heard some scuffling. Then…

"Stop, Char. I'm in love with Gloria."

Gloria fell back against the wall. He loved her? She covered her mouth.

"And I realize what I felt for you was *never* love."

Char laughed, a derisive sound. "You're so stupid." Boots paced across the floor. "He knew, you know." Her voice became bitchy. "I told Kenny what happened. He knew everything."

"Get out." Dillon's voice was low and dangerous. "Go find some other man to suck dry."

"You're an ass, Dillon Cross."

"I know. And Kenny deserved better than you."

Gloria heard the sound of a palm laid hard against a cheek. Then stomping footsteps and a slamming door. She stayed where she was, leaning against the wall, breathing heavy.

"Gloria? You can come out now."

Shit.

Was it wrong to be smiling at a time like this? Not that

she could contain it, even when she saw Dillon's stricken features. She stopped behind one of the new sofas, needing some distance between herself and the man she loved.

"You heard the whole thing?"

"Yes."

He took a couple steps toward her and stopped. "You were never a bet. I mean, I had a bet with Jamie—just some stupid guy shit—but, it meant nothing and—"

"I know."

"You do?"

"Yes." She took a few steps forward, meeting him half-way. "I'm not stupid."

"I know. You're the smartest person I've ever met."

She took another step. Stopped. "Can I say something?"

Dillon stayed where he was. "Of course."

One more step and she was within touching distance, but she didn't touch. "Whatever happened between you and Char? When she was married to Kenny? That wasn't your fault."

"You don't know that."

"Oh, yes, I do." She inched closer. "That woman is a mountain lion. She stalks and then she pounces."

Dillon's lips twitched and Gloria felt hers respond in kind. "Now," she said, waving to the back of the house. "I've got two horses saddled and waiting out back. Let's you and me go for a ride."

THIS TIME GLORIA led the way and Dillon followed, though it didn't take long for him to figure out where they were going as they navigated through a narrow section of creek and began the ascent up the familiar slope, the moon lighting their way. Stars greeted them as they crested the hill and, side by side, rode up to the Doghouse. She dismounted first, tied up the horse, climbed the steps and sat down on the porch swing.

"Are you gonna join me or you just gonna sit there?"

The woman was bossy and he loved her for it.

After dismounting and climbing up to the porch, he settled himself on the swing beside her, removing his hat and running a hand through his hair.

"You're not selling the ranch," she said, matter-of-fact.

"I'm not?"

"No."

His lips twisted in a smile.

"I know there's an offer, but you're not going to take it. You love this place and you have to keep it."

"You think you know my mind better than me?"

She tilted her face up. "Maybe." She smiled.

"Okay, how about I make you a deal?" He brushed a strand of hair away from her eyes.

She wrinkled that cute little nose of hers. "O-kay," she said slowly.

"I won't sell, if you agree to stay."

She grinned wide, tapping her lips. "That sounds like blackmail."

He put his arm around her and pulled her in nice and close, right where she fit perfectly. "Well, I figure I'm allowed a little blackmail after you orchestrated this whole thing tonight with Char."

She threw her head back against his arm and laughed. He loved how free and spontaneous she was. "I did kind of set you up, didn't I?"

"You did."

"When did you figure it out?"

"When I saw Sage's truck out the side window, heard horses whinnying out back."

She reached up and touched his jaw, rubbing the backs

of her knuckles against his whiskers the way he loved. "Okay, cowboy. I'll stay."

He grabbed her hand and squeezed. "You sure?"

"Of course I'm sure." She crawled on top of him, resting a knee on either side of his legs. "I'd only pull a *Sue* for the man I love."

He groaned. Those words sounded so good to his ears. "I love you so damn much, Red."

"Good." She rested her palms on either side of his face, gazing deeply into his eyes. "Dillon?"

"Yeah, babe?"

"Kiss me."

"That, I can do."

GLORIA STARED AT the low rafters of the loft, lying contentedly within Dillon's embrace, her head on his shoulder as he stroked her hair.

"You sure you're not gonna find it too boring out here in the middle of nowhere?" he asked quietly.

She nestled herself against him. "I'm lying here in this tiny loft with the man I love. What more could I possibly want?"

"I don't know." His hand stilled. "Your friends? Your condo? Your life back in Chicago?"

"I can visit."

"What about your dad?"

She rolled onto his chest, propped her chin on her hands so she was only a couple inches from him. "It took me a while to figure out, but my dad's a grown man. I have to let him live his life. Wherever that is and in whatever way he sees fit." She sucked on her lip, not caring that she was doing it. "I love him, but he's not my responsibility."

"Well, he and Sage looked mighty cozy on the dance floor earlier." Dillon resumed his gentle stroking.

"I saw that."

"You know, it was when I danced with you that I knew I had to have you." Dillon's voice took on a deeper, sexier tone as he tugged on her hair.

"Really?"

"Yes, ma'am."

She rubbed her cheek against his chest and whispered, "You know when I knew?"

"Nope."

"When you sang." She lifted her face. "At the wedding. I was like, my God, I want that man to sing to me."

"Is that right?"

"Yes, sir," she said, playfully adopting his easy drawl.

"Well, what's a man to do with that information?"

She drew a circle on his chest. "Dunno, though you're a smart guy, I'm sure you can figure it out."

He pulled her right up close, her head beneath his chin, and smoothed her hair. Then, he started to sing. "*Looking back on the memory of the dance we shared 'neath the stars above...*"

Only her all-time favorite country song, "The Dance" by Garth Brooks.

Gloria closed her eyes listening to the sound of his voice as it came from deep inside his chest, and she smiled because, unlike the sad lyrics in the song, she wasn't ever going to say goodbye to Dillon.

Nope.

She loved him and this was where she could breathe, where she felt free for the first time, where she belonged.

This was home.

* * * * *

#895 COWBOY ALL NIGHT
Thunder Mountain Brotherhood
by Vicki Lewis Thompson

When Aria Danes hires a legendary horse trainer to work with her new foal, she isn't expecting sexy, easygoing Brant Ellison. But when they're together, it's too hot for either to maintain their cool!

#896 A SEAL'S DESIRE
Uniformly Hot!
by Tawny Weber

Petty Officer Christian "Cowboy" Laramie is the hero Sammie Jo Wilson always looked up to. When she needs his help, she finds out she is the only woman Laramie thinks is off-limits...but for how long?

#897 TURNING UP THE HEAT
Friends With Benefits
by Tanya Michaels

Pastry chef Phoebe Mars and sophisticated charmer Heath Jensen are only pretending to date in order to make Phoebe's ex jealous. But there's nothing pretend about the sexy heat between them!

#898 IN THE BOSS'S BED
by J. Margot Critch

Separating business and pleasure proves to be impossible for Maya Connor and Jamie Sellers. When they can't keep their passion out of the boardroom, scandal threatens to destroy everything they've worked for.

---

*Aria Danes puts her dreams on hold to help her
injured brother. A foal will be just the therapy he needs.
But when she meets horse trainer Brant Ellison,
the chemistry between them may derail all her
carefully laid plans...!*

Read on for a sneak preview of
COWBOY ALL NIGHT, *the first story of 2016*
in New York Times *bestselling author*
Vicki Lewis Thompson's sexy cowboy saga
THUNDER MOUNTAIN BROTHERHOOD.

He longed to reach for her, but instead he leaned into the
van and snagged her hat. "You'll need this."

"Thanks." She settled the hat on her head—instant
sexy cowgirl. "Let's go."

Somehow he managed to stop looking at her long
enough to put his feet in motion. No doubt about it, he
was hooked on her, and they'd only met yesterday.

If she was aware of his infatuation, she didn't let on
as they walked into the barn. "I'm excited that we'll be
taking him out today. I thought he might have to stay
inside a little longer."

"Only if the weather had been nasty. But it's
gorgeous." Like *you.* He'd almost said that out loud. Talk
about cheesy compliments. "Cade and I already turned
the other horses out into the far pasture, but we kept
these two in the barn. We figured you should be here for
Linus's big moment."

"Thank goodness you waited for me. I would have been crushed if I'd missed this."

"I wouldn't have let that happen." Okay, he was grandstanding a little, but it was true. Nobody at the ranch would have allowed Aria to miss watching Linus experience his first time outside.

"How about Rosie and Herb? Will they come watch?"

"You couldn't keep them away. A foal's first day in the pasture is special. Lexi and Cade are up at the house having breakfast with them, so they'll all come down in a bit." And he'd text them so they'd know she was here.

But not yet. He didn't foresee a lot of opportunities to be alone with her unless he created them. He wanted to savor this moment for a little while longer.

"Brant, can I ask a favor?" She paused and turned to him.

"Sure." He stopped walking.

Taking off her hat, she stepped toward him. "Would you please kiss me?"

With a groan he swept her up into his arms so fast she squeaked in surprise and his hat fell off…again. His mouth found hers and he thrust his tongue deep. His hands slid around her and when he lifted her up, she gave a little hop and wrapped her legs around his hips. Dear God, it felt good to wedge himself between her thighs.

Don't miss COWBOY ALL NIGHT
by New York Times *bestselling author*
Vicki Lewis Thompson, available June 2016 wherever
Harlequin® Blaze® books and ebooks are sold.

www.Harlequin.com

HBEXP0516

Whatever You're Into... Passionate Reads

Looking for more passionate reads from Harlequin®?
Fear not! Harlequin® Presents, Harlequin® Desire and
Harlequin® Blaze offer you irresistible romance stories
featuring powerful heroes.

HARLEQUIN *Presents*

Do you want alpha males, decadent glamour and jet-set
lifestyles? Step into the sensational, sophisticated world of
Harlequin® Presents, where sinfully tempting heroes ignite a
fierce and wickedly irresistible passion!

HARLEQUIN *Desire*

Harlequin® Desire novels are powerful, passionate and
provocative contemporary romances set against a backdrop of
wealth, privilege and sweeping family saga. Alpha heroes with
a soft side meet strong-willed but vulnerable heroines amid a
dramatic world of divided loyalties, high-stakes conflict and
intense emotion.

HARLEQUIN *Blaze*

Harlequin® Blaze stories sizzle with strong heroines and
irresistible heroes playing the game of modern love and lust.
They're fun, sexy and always steamy.

Be sure to check out our full selection of books
within each series every month!

www.Harlequin.com

Reading Has Its Rewards

Earn **FREE BOOKS!**

Register at **Harlequin My Rewards** and submit your Harlequin purchases from wherever you shop to earn points for free books and other exclusive rewards.

Plus submit your purchases from now till May 30th for a chance to win a $500 Visa Card*.

Visit **HarlequinMyRewards.com** today

MYR16R1